JUNKYARD MAN

A LOCUST POINT MYSTERY

LIBBY HOWARD

CHAPTER 1

The pumps fired up with a whir of sound and a whoosh of water. I cheered like I'd just witnessed a Hail Mary pass at a Locust Point High School football game. The hot tub repair man wiped a hand across his forehead and grinned at me. "Wasn't sure I'd be able to get this going, Mrs. Carrera. These things sit for too long and the pumps seize up."

I'd had no idea. After an entire day of scrubbing the inside of a hot tub, rubber gloves up to my elbows, knee-deep in cleaning spray and some anti-mold stuff, I'd happily filled my sparkling clean hot tub and turned it on to…nothing. Thankfully Sweenie's Pool and Spa took pity on my frantic pleas for help and sent Franc out to work his magic on my pumps.

"Thank you so much, Franc. Did I get the chemicals right?" It had been a huge worry for me. I'd tested pH and did all the little test strips, measuring the different chemicals carefully. This had always been Eli's thing. After the accident, I'd muddled along for a few years before draining the hot tub and throwing in the towel. Taking care of an invalid husband didn't allow much time for things like maintaining a hot tub that no one used.

He grinned. "I took care of it, Mrs. C."

I looked into the frothing water highlighted with blue and purple lights. When we'd bought this thing, it had been top of the line, insanely expensive. We'd had money to spare, and there had been many nights when Eli and I had relaxed in this tub, letting the stresses of the day fall away. Most nights, we'd wound up making out like teenagers, giggling and running inside to make love, still damp and warm, just inside the back door.

And now I was revitalizing this hot tub so that two teenagers could enjoy a quick dip after finishing their homework.

Franc got to work on the invoice while I surveyed my yard. The herb garden was clean and neat, and the spot for my little vegetable garden had been tilled courtesy of my neighbor Will Lars. I had a dozen packets of seeds, peat pots, starter soil, and cheap aluminum roasting trays to hold my seedlings until the weather was warm enough to plant.

"Is it working? It's working! Madison, it's working!" Henry was nearly dancing with excitement. He eyed me hopefully.

"Finish your homework?" I asked. He nodded enthusiastically. "Then make sure it's okay with your dad and get your suit on."

He ran into the house past Madison who was sitting at the patio table, a laptop and several heavy textbooks spread out in front of her. I felt bad for the girl. Her homework was nearly double Henry's. I wasn't sure she'd get done in time to squeeze in a bit of a hot tub swim. Maybe I could ask her father, Judge Beck, if she could stay up a bit late. Or maybe she could have a couple of friends over and we'd do a pizza and hot tub party this weekend.

"Here you go, Mrs. C." Franc handed me the invoice. I grimaced when I read the amount. Judge Beck's rent payment covered my mortgage, leaving my paycheck for food, utilities, and other luxuries. This wasn't in the budget, but I couldn't disappoint the kids, and after all my work cleaning this thing, I didn't want to just let it sit and get moldy. I'd need to cut back here and there to pay this one.

"Thirty days, Mrs. C." Franc smiled knowingly at me. In a small town like Locust Point, there were no secrets. Well, there were secrets like that our mayor was a murderer and one of his victims, a young successful party-planner, was running a prostitution ring. But my secret, that I was flat broke after my husband's death, wasn't.

"Eli was a good man, Mrs. C. You need anything, you let me know, okay?"

I felt the sting of tears. Eli *had* been a good man. I missed him. I missed the man I'd married as well as the man he'd become after the accident. "Thank you, Franc. I appreciate it."

He grinned, gathering up his tool bag and heading down my walkway to his truck. "Call me if you have any other issues. We guarantee our work."

I smiled, knowing that he meant they especially guaranteed their work on *my* hot tub.

After Franc left, I wandered over to Madison, stooping to pick up my tabby and running a hand along the thick fur of his back.

"What have you gotten into, Taco?" I asked the cat. His fur was sticky and smudged with something dark. I'd need to bathe him, and there was nothing Taco hated more than a bath.

Madison wrinkled her nose. "He's been going over to the place across the street. I see him over there when I get back from school."

Ugh. I had nothing against Mr. Peter, but his lawn was like a junkyard, and his house inside wasn't much better from what I'd heard. He had a soft spot for cats and dogs and was known for putting out food for strays. I was pretty sure he was slipping Taco some scraps on a daily basis to encourage regular visits. And given the diet I'd put my cat on a few weeks ago, Taco wouldn't say 'no' to supplemental meals. Actually, even without the diet, Taco wouldn't say 'no' to supplemental meals.

I'd need to go talk to my neighbor and ask him to lay off the treats. Taco really did need to lose weight, and obviously there was something over there he was rubbing against. There were only so many baths I could give my kitty before he ditched me and permanently moved in with Mr. Peter. And as much as my neighbor would probably like that, I wasn't going to give up my cat.

"What have you got going on there, Madison?" I put Taco down and leaned over her shoulder. "Chemistry. Hmmm."

"It's an AP class." The girl chewed on the tip of her pen. "I don't think I have a future in biochemistry."

"It's good to explore different options. How else are you going to know what you might want to have as a career—and what you know you absolutely don't want to have as a career."

"How did you know you wanted to be a journalist?" she asked.

I was a skip tracer now working for a bail bondsman/private investigator, but until Eli's accident I'd been a journalist. I'd still be a journalist if it was a viable career, but in today's world, news stories were purchased in bulk or acquired from freelancers making forty dollars an article. So, I'd turned my talent for research and fact checking to a field that might actually pay my bills.

"I worked on our high school newsletter and was a

member of the yearbook committee and loved it. In college I thought I might want to be a novelist or maybe teach English, but creative writing wasn't my strength and my short stint as a professor's assistant made it clear that teaching wasn't my strength, either."

"Well, chemistry isn't my strength," she grumbled. "And biology wasn't much better."

I pulled out a chair and sat next to her. "So what *is* your strength?"

She shrugged. "I'd always wanted to be a doctor, but I'm beginning to think that's a bad idea."

If she wasn't fond of biology or chemistry, then she was right. "What do you like? Maybe you can be a lawyer like your father."

"Ugh, no." She wrinkled her nose. "He worked crazy hours even before he was a judge. We barely saw him when we were little. As much as I hate this divorce, Dad spends more time with us now than he ever had before. I don't want that kind of life."

I leaned back in the chair. "What kind of life *do* you want?"

"Time for softball in the evenings and weekends. A job I really love, but one that lets me have space for a husband and my kids. I want to be able to go with them for a week at the beach, and weekends skiing, and to their birthday parties and…all that."

My heart ached. Madison loved her father, that much was clear from the short time I'd known them. She loved him and acutely felt every missed moment that his career had cost them. But a teen didn't always understand the joy of losing yourself in the passion of a career that didn't end at five o'clock. And children didn't always understand that in a marriage, sometimes one partner sacrifices time with their family to be the provider, and the other sacrifices a career and financial independence to be the primary parent.

Henry came dashing out, bright plaid patterned swim trunks on and a towel over his shoulder. Judge Beck followed him, eyeing the hot tub. "It's ready, Kay? Doesn't it need to sit a bit and let the chemicals...I don't know, settle or something?"

I smiled, watching Henry toss his towel on a chair and scramble into the tub. "It's ready. Well, it's more of a luke-warm tub than a hot tub at the moment, but I don't think your son minds."

No, he didn't. The boy had leaned back against the head-rest, his feet stretching out above the water toward one of the jets. "Someone bring me a piña colada. And some ice cream."

Madison snorted. "This isn't the Hilton. If you're thirsty, go get a juice box."

Judge Beck looked down at the girl's textbook, reaching out a hand to tousle her hair. "Almost done, honey?"

She smiled up at him and my heart swelled to see the affection exchanged in their glance. "No. I've probably got another hour at least. Once I'm done with this, I need to do some research for a Civics essay."

The judge winced. "Can you take a break? Miss Carrera went to a lot of trouble to get this hot tub running for you two."

She looked longingly over at her brother, lounging in the churning water. "I'd be up 'til midnight if I did. I'll get in another night."

"When it's actually hot," I added. "Maybe your dad will let you have a few friends over this weekend to have pizza and get in the spa."

Her eyes lit up, then her face fell. "We both have games

Friday night and then there is another one for me on Saturday morning, and Henry in the afternoon."

And Sunday was for family. I got how Judge Beck was trying to keep one day to actually bond with his kids, especially now that the hectic sports schedules ate up what wasn't earmarked for schoolwork. With him and Heather splitting custody, their Sunday family time had become more like every other Sunday.

Judge Beck looked over at the hot tub, then back down at his daughter. "Henry would have to have a couple of friends over too. That's a lot in your hot tub, Kay."

Madison wrinkled her nose, and I knew exactly what she was thinking. It wouldn't nearly be as much fun having a few girlfriends over if her younger brother and his friends were gawking at them and making fart jokes the whole evening.

"Maybe Madison can have two or three of her softball teammates over after the game on Saturday. I'll play hostess and you can spend some one-on-one time with Henry after his game. Then in two weeks, when you have the kids for the weekend again, we'll switch and I'll entertain Henry and his friends while you do something with Madison."

"We could go to the mall together," the girl teased her father.

The judge's eyes widened with horror, then he laughed. "All right. Madison, no more than four friends, okay? You really don't mind, Kay?"

I'd just spent a bunch of money getting this hot tub fixed up. Might as well put it to good use. Besides, it felt good to hear footsteps in the house, to hear the sound of laughter and conversation. Eli and I had always loved parties, and we'd made a habit of entertaining weekly. After his accident, the house had grown silent and I'd forgotten how uplifting the presence of others could be in my home. A house this big deserved to be filled with life, lighting up the dark corners and chasing away all the old ghosts.

"I don't mind at all."

Madison pumped both fists up and down in excitement "Yesssss. I'll send some texts just as soon as I'm done with this chapter."

The girl had been working so hard the past few months, trying to regain her parents' trust after she'd been caught at a party drinking beer with much older kids—one of whom had been the woman who'd been running the prostitution ring. I wasn't sure Judge Beck was ready to let her go to sleepovers or out with friends yet, but this supervised party would reward Madison for her squeaky clean behavior the past few months.

I watched Taco roll in the dirt and winced. "You kids haven't been slipping Taco any extra treats, have you?"

Both of them denied it.

"I think Mr. Peter from across the street is feeding him," Henry called out over the noise of the hot tub. "The house with the appliances, and tires, and old mattresses in the front yard."

"Mr. Lars was yelling at him yesterday when I was getting the mail," Madison added. "Told the Junkyard Man that his place was a fire hazard."

It probably was, although Will Lars hadn't been quite as vocal about it until he and his wife decided to turn their house into a Bed and Breakfast Inn. Will and Kat weren't the only ones who were frustrated with Mr. Peter's hoarding tendencies. Every time someone put their house on the market, they complained about the eyesore. Petitions hadn't helped. Calling the city and the county hadn't helped. One neighbor had tried to get the property condemned without success. Each year the junk pile grew, but Locust Point was a small town and Mr. Peter was a bit of a fixture here. I hated seeing the mess right across the street from me, but over the years I'd learned to ignore it.

"I'm sure his name isn't Junkyard Man," Judge Beck scolded. "Nicknames like that aren't amusing, Madison."

She blushed red. "I don't know his name. And you don't want to know what Mr. Lars was calling him."

I'm sure he didn't.

"His name is Harry Peter," I told the girl.

Silence greeted my words. Then Madison giggled, and Henry burst out laughing. Even Judge Beck quickly hid a smile behind a frown. "Harold Peter," he corrected.

"No, actually, his first name is Harry. And he's quite proud of it." Harry Peter. I'd laughed myself breathless the first few times I'd heard what the poor man's mother had saddled him with, but after all these years it hardly elicited a smile anymore.

"Is it really hairy?" Henry choked out between laughs. "Dillon's mom told him if he spent too much time—"

"Henry, that's enough," Judge Beck scolded. "You kids will call the neighbor across the street Mr. Peter, and if I hear anything different, you'll be grounded. Got it?"

"Got it," both kids chimed.

"Well, I'm going to have a chat with Mr. Peter," I told them. "Because he's sabotaging my cat's diet."

Our road was lined with big old Victorian and Queen Anne-style homes with varying accents on the same basic theme. Mine had a corner turret with gingerbread trim and was full of sharp angles. Mr. Peter's had pointed dormers and a jutting glass-enclosed side porch that was filled to the ceiling with cardboard boxes and plastic bins overflowing with dinnerware and paper goods. The Larses' house was right next door, the mirror image of Mr. Peter's house without all the junk. And their elegant porch had been made into a lovely breakfast nook—with a less-than-lovely view of

Mr. Peter's eighty rolls of toilet paper and cardboard boxes. And three plungers.

I paused to regard the plungers. Generally, when one needed such a device, it was an emergency, and thus it was important to keep these things right next to the toilet. They would be less than useful all the way in the enclosed porch behind dozens of boxes. Perhaps these were spares.

Turning away from the porch, I made my way through the maze of old appliances, automotive parts, rusted lawn-mowers, and piles of half-rotted lumber to the front door, noting that in spite of the clutter, the porch was sound and appeared to be freshly painted. There was the sound of foot-steps at my knock, and one of the narrow wooden doors squawked open to reveal a trim man in his early eighties with a tobacco-stained silver beard and dark brown eyes.

"Hello, Mr. Peter. I'm Kay Carrera from across the street."

"I know." His voice was gruff, no doubt from the same tobacco that had yellowed his beard. "Sorry to hear about your husband."

I'd gotten a condolence card from him just before Eli's funeral. I'd been touched that a neighbor I rarely saw had thought to send his sympathies. Maybe it was my fault that I didn't see Mr. Peter very often. His yard gave the impression that he wouldn't welcome visitors, but that might have been far from the truth. Not that it had crossed my mind to share a cup of tea with this man in his junk-filled house.

Mr. Peter stood aside, holding the door open. "Come in. Would you like some tea?"

"Oh, no thank you." I did step inside though, filled with curiosity to see what the inside of his house looked like.

It looked pretty much like the outside of his house. I couldn't see anything past that main parlor because it was stacked floor-to-ceiling with boxes, a narrow path winding its way toward what I thought might be the kitchen. To the right stood a broad staircase, made nearly impassable by stacks of books and old newspapers. To the left, the entrance to the enclosed porch was blocked by two large shelving units lined with little china vases and crystal plates. Across the top was a long decorative sword. I eyed it, hoping it didn't fall and cut one of us.

"You sure you don't want some tea? I just put the kettle on."

The house was claustrophobic, overloaded with stuff, the boxes coated in dust, the ceiling cracked, the floor scuffed and gouged. Mr. Peter must have spent his little cleaning time on the contents of the shelving units because the pretty little china vases and plates were sparkling. It wasn't quite as bad as I'd imagined, though. I'd expected horrible smells, dead animals sticking out from carelessly placed rags, a floor two feet under layers of stuff. Don't get me wrong, Mr. Peter was a hoarder, and the house had to be violating all sorts of fire codes, but there was a narrow pathway around the boxes, and it actually smelled like someone's attic—a sort of dust-and-mothballs-and old boxes smell.

"Honestly, I can't stay. I just came to apologize for my cat's trespass on your property and ask if you could please not feed him if he wanders over again. He's getting so fat, and the diet I have him on isn't working when he's begging food off the neighbors."

This was really my own darned fault. I needed to keep Taco inside and not let him wander the block like this. I hated the thought that he might be hit by my paper-man on his early morning delivery route, or one of the neighbors coming home late from work. And it really wasn't fair that my cat was trotting across people's lawns, annoying their dogs and possibly hunting down their songbirds.

"I'm going to try to keep him inside the house from now on," I vowed. "It's hard because he yowls his head off to go out, and I know he'll probably sneak through the door on occasion. Can you call me if he comes over? And not feed him?"

"Oh, but I love the Taco-schmacko." Mr. Peter reached out and took my fat-and-dirty cat from my arms. "There's a good boy. He comes and visits me every day and shares my chicken sandwiches. I'll miss my little buddy's visits."

Well, the chicken sandwiches were probably the reason why Taco visited every day, but the cat did seem very fond of Mr. Peter, rubbing his head across the man's beard and purring loud enough that I was sure people two blocks away could hear him.

"Maybe you could get a cat of your own." But then I looked around at the condition of the house and reconsidered the idea. Yes, it was cleaner and somewhat more organized than I'd thought, but I could just envision a cat jumping from stack of boxes to stack of boxes and getting stuck behind a bunch of them to slowly starve to death.

"I've considered it, but cats knock things over, and I've got a lot of precious stuff in this house."

Precious cases of toilet paper and tissue? Although those vases on the shelves were pretty.

"Taco-schmacko doesn't break stuff. Do you boy? Do you boy?" he cooed to my cat.

I wasn't sure what bothered me more, his nickname for my cat or the fact that he was using baby talk and smooshing his face into Taco's fur. He was right, though. Taco wasn't the sort of cat who pushed china off tables, knocked over wine glasses, or pooped in the potted plants. I think some of that might have been that he was fat, and all that took effort— effort that was better spent begging for food.

"He's gained a lot of weight the last three months," I told him. Then I reached out and took my cat back. "Please just call me if he comes back? And please don't feed him?"

Mr. Peter's smile was more than a bit sad. "Okay. I'll miss him."

And now I felt like a horrible person. Yes, his house was cluttered to the point that I was on the edge of a panic attack, but he seemed to be a nice guy, and he clearly had a genuine regard for Taco. I'd lived here for thirty years and hadn't spoken more than a dozen words to him the whole time. I'd rarely seen visitors, only someone I thought might have been a nephew.

"I'm hoping to have a neighborhood cookout soon." As in, I was thinking about it right now and hadn't been planning it for more than the last two seconds. "I'll send you an invitation. Or maybe you could come over for a glass of wine on the porch with Daisy and me Friday evening?"

"I don't leave the house anymore. My knee. And the arthritis in my hip…" His eyes lit up. "Do you think you could bring something by sometime, though? There was a beautiful nineteenth-century Rorstrand pitcher you had in the front window a few years back that I always admired. I'd love to see it up close."

I had no idea what he was talking about. "The one with the gold lacy pattern and flowers? Or the leaves?"

"The gold and flowers. I'm a fan of Faience, French and Northern Italian mostly, although some of the Polish patterns are quite attractive. They're far more readily available."

No. Idea. "Is that what the vases are on the shelf up front?"

He beamed. "My newest pieces, although I have some of the rarer ones stored up in the bedroom including some fourteenth-century Majolica." A wary expression crossed his face. "None of it is all that valuable. Junk really. Because everything here is junk."

Two seconds ago, I would have believed that. But Mr.

Peter had nothing to fear from me. I didn't want his pretty pottery, and as cash-strapped as I was, I'd never stoop to stealing.

"Value is in the eye of the beholder, isn't it?"

He nodded. "And in my eyes, every item in this house is priceless."

"Even the cases of toilet paper?"

He grinned. "Even the cases of toilet paper."

I picked my way back through the maze of a path, hoping none of the boxes, or that darned sword, fell down on my head. Then I wished Mr. Peter a good evening and headed across the street, a pudgy purring Taco in my arms. The light was dimming. Madison was typing on her laptop and taking notes. Henry had climbed out of the hot tub and wrapped a towel around himself. He tucked the end in at his waist and reached up to flip the lid over the spa, sliding his feet into a pair of sneakers. The golden lights came on in the garden area, bathing the backyard with ambient light. I heard the clank of pots and pans through the open kitchen window against a backdrop of insect song. My home. And it was so much more of a home now that I wasn't here alone.

A shadow moved by the porch, approaching and falling in beside me. Taco squirmed in my arms and I reluctantly let him down, knowing he'd be meowing at the door in five minutes wanting his dinner. As the cat darted off into the bushes with an irritated growl, the shadow drew closer. It felt cool by my side, a dark blur just in the corner of my vision.

"Dinner!" Judge Beck called.

Henry hustled inside. "Give me five to put some clothes on."

Madison grumbled under her breath and snapped the laptop lid closed, gathering up her notebooks and pencils. "Coming."

I watched her trot up the stairs and in the back door. I listened to the quiet murmur of their voices, the clink of their dishes as they ate. Taco raced by, chasing a bug. I sat in the glider, and the shadow sat down beside me, leaning back into the cushions as I rocked us back and forth.

The shadow was rarely around during the day, and occasionally in the afternoon, but he had become my constant companion in the night hours. He was near as I watched movies on the basement entertainment center. He was by my side on evening walks, or as I sat in the backyard garden. Sometimes as I slept, I could feel him near, even though in the darkness I couldn't see him. And if I ate dinner alone, as I often did to give Judge Beck and his children their private time, he sat to my right.

And the shadow was a he, of that I was sure.

"It's a beautiful evening. I'm glad I got the hot tub fixed. The kids are going to have such fun with it. And I do want to have that neighborhood barbeque. Maybe next Friday evening when the kids have their games. It will be an adult party with wine and cigars, like Eli and I used to host before the accident." I thought for a moment. "No. That was the past. That isn't something I can recapture. I'll schedule it on an evening when the kids will be here and that way the neighbors can meet them. That way Judge Beck and his family can start to feel like they're truly part of the neighborhood."

The shadow didn't reply. He never did. But I still got the impression that he approved.

CHAPTER 2

"Annnnnd, cut!"

The command would have been far more dramatic had J.T. himself not been manning the tiny camera that he'd unboxed just last week. And it would have been a whole lot more entertaining had he not been filming me.

My boss had given up on the dream of A&E knocking at his door with a contract for a reality show based on his private investigation company. Actually, he'd never truly given up that dream, he'd just decided that the road there included producing his own "wildly successful'" YouTube channel. This detour was being assisted by two Sony hand-held video cameras and a pair of tripods that J.T. had picked up from the local pawnshop.

My boss scooted the cameras around, positioning them and fussing over the settings. "The next scene is you taking the call that the perp has skipped town. Ready, Kay?"

I was ready. And I was thrilled that this was my last on-camera appearance for the day before J.T. downloaded the files and pieced everything together for his big internet debut. The perp had indeed skipped town—yesterday. And he'd been caught over in Milford, high as a kite. J.T. had already filmed the reenactment of that less-than-dramatic apprehension but felt that editing in some other scenes would help create the correct mood. Thus, he now had footage of me as his computer wiz assistant, and several shots of slamming jail cell doors and stern-looking police officers.

Our local PD were as thrilled with the venture and every one of them wanted their moment of fame. Once J.T. loaded the file, I was willing to bet nearly every cop in the county would be watching the video, enlarging frames to see if they'd made it to the big screen or wound up on the cutting room floor.

"Roll 'em!"

I picked up the phone, trying for my best forties gumshoe detective expression, then I widened my eyes in shock and slammed the phone down, spinning my chair around to face the camera. "Gator! We got a problem! Our guy is in the wind!"

"Cut!"

J.T., aka Gator, beamed at me. "That was awesome, Kay. Although we need to think of a cool nickname for you, too. Kay is so…"

It was so 1950s. But I really didn't want J.T. to saddle me with some ridiculous nickname like "Snap" or "Hawk".. Gator kind of worked for him, although the nearest gator was a hundred miles away and that one was in a zoo.

"Am I good to get back to work now? I've got three Credicorp cases, and I need to get addresses for the filings by the end of the week."

The drug addict who'd jumped bail for all of two hours was exciting, but my skip-tracing work was what really brought in steady income for the company. Unfortunately, finding people who'd run out on their credit card or hospital bills wasn't exactly prime-time worthy.

"Yep. It'll take me a while to edit all this and upload it. Ooh, do you think I need a soundtrack? Can you find me some copyright-free music? Open source stuff?"

"Can you pay me overtime?" I muttered under my breath. "Yeah, sure." Those words were loud enough for my boss to hear.

I looked up a few sites and e-mailed J.T. the links, then got to work while listening to him grumble in the background over poor lighting and blurry shots.

It was an hour before quitting time when I finally heard him whoop with success. An e-mail with a link popped up on my screen. I sighed and put aside my work to watch it, ensuring that J.T. now had one view on his YouTube channel.

It actually wasn't half bad. All those years of watching seventies and eighties detective shows plus his reality show fixation must have imprinted in J.T.'s mind because his "Gator, Private Eye" was a heck of a lot better than those knitting videos I'd been watching in the evenings.

"Nice job, J.T.," I told him.

He beamed, rubbing a hand over his ultra-short, silver hair. He'd given up on the shaved, bald look, claiming that remembering to put sunscreen on his scalp at the golf course was problematic.

"Thanks." His grin turned sly. "I hear you've got some drama of your own over in your neighborhood."

J.T. was a gossip. In some ways, he was worse than my friend and neighbor, Daisy. And I had no idea what he was talking about. Drama to J.T. could be anything from a shocking domestic violence report to a trip-and-fall at the block yard sale.

"Which drama are you referring to?" I knew he'd tell me. J.T. always told me.

"Lars is trying to sic the city health inspector on Harry Peter." He laughed. "It sounds like we're about to have a venereal disease epidemic. I can never keep a straight face when I say that man's name."

I ignored J.T.'s little joke. "Will Lars is frustrated. I get it. He's trying to open a bed and breakfast. Property taxes are up. He got laid off the end of last year and it's tough making it on Kat's income alone. Customers don't want to pull up to a swank, restored Victorian house and see a junkyard next door."

My boss shook his head, still chuckling over the VD joke. "Honestly, Lars just needs to wait a few years. Peter is what… ninety? He'll probably drop dead before the summer is over."

"He's early eighties by my guess. And everyone has been waiting for him to drop dead for the last twenty years. Personally, I think the guy will outlive us all."

J.T. stood and walked over to hover by my desk. "You live across the street from the guy. What do you think Lars's chances are?"

I sniffed. "Slim to none. The Millers tried the same thing fifteen years ago when they were trying to sell and Peter's place was driving down their property value. Say what you will about Peter's eccentricities, but he does minimally maintain the house and property."

Of course, it was pretty easy to minimally maintain the property when there were appliances covering every square inch of what used to be grass. No mowing or weed-eating necessary. And what happened on the inside was his business as the property owner. I doubted they'd condemn the place if it had a leaking roof and a non-working furnace since it was owner occupied.

"That was fifteen years ago. There's got to be something that's happened since then—black mold, dead rats, rotted bananas. Or maybe fire hazards? The city can do something if there are no clear paths for the fire department if the place goes up in flames, right?"

I sighed and leaned back in my chair. "It's not that simple, J.T. The city can cite him for code infractions, but he'd have thirty, or sixty, or ninety days to correct them, and there are usually extensions upon extensions. If the building isn't on the verge of collapse, if it's not in a condition that endangers neighbors or pedestrians on the sidewalk, then they probably won't push the issue."

"Black mold?" J.T. repeated. "Dead rats?"

Oh, for Pete's sake. "I was just in there yesterday. I didn't smell any dead animals, or mold, or even rotted bananas."

"He let you in?" J.T.'s eyes widened. "What was it like?"

I squirmed, reluctant to discuss the details of my neighbor's obsessive collecting tendencies. "It was like a house—a house with a lot of stuff."

I turned to get back to my work, noticing out of the corner of my eye that J.T. was still hovering.

"What about the lawn? All those appliances? All that junk?"

I rolled my eyes. "We don't have an HOA. If he wants to have a front lawn full of old washing machines, there's nothing stopping him. Daisy has dream catchers and an altar in her yard. The Sedgewicks have half a dozen plastic flamingos. Every Christmas, Bob Simmons puts every inflatable ornament known to mankind around his house. I can't even *see* his house when they're all blown up. It's a slippery slope, J.T. You don't want the government removing you from your house because the neighbors don't like your shutters or basketball hoop or ornamental gazing sphere. You don't want the government removing you from your house because someone thinks your comic collection or dozen cats or strict adherence to Feng Shui means you're ready to be involuntarily committed. There's always a risk that someone's pink flamingos, or Wiccan altar or washing-machine covered front lawn is going to affect your house value. That doesn't override their right to enjoy their property in any manner they see fit as long as it doesn't affect public health."

I should have gotten an Academy Award for that speech. Maybe posing for J.T.'s videos had turned me into an actress.

"Ah, well. Guess Lars will just have to wait for old man Peter to drop dead, then." J.T. turned around and grabbed his briefcase off a chair. "It's Friday, Kay. Take off early and go to happy hour or something. You can get back to those on Monday."

Easy for him to say. He wouldn't be the one with a pile of work on his desk first thing Monday morning. I hated leaving for the weekend with unfinished business, It followed me around, haunted me, loomed at the edge of my awareness just like that darned shadow in my vision. But at this rate I'd be here until sunset, and I'd been looking forward to wine-on-the-porch night with Daisy.

"Thanks." I waved J.T. out the door and stuffed the folders into my bag, just in case I couldn't take it and had to work on them over the weekend. Then I turned off the lights, locked the door, and headed home.

CHAPTER 3

"See? The purl stitch has the textured loop facing, where the knit stitch is smooth."

"Just like on a sweater," I commented, flipping the swatch back and forth in amazement. After struggling for months with the instructions that came with my knitting kit and online videos, I finally decided that I'd never progress beyond lumpy, glue-finished, polygon-shaped washcloths without some one-on-one help. I truly wanted to make hats for the hospital maternity ward and other donation-worthy items, but I hadn't even perfected the washcloth. Actually, it was so far from perfect that I was ashamed to use them myself, let alone torture some poor unfortunate with my terrible handiwork.

Suzette picked up the sample I'd been working on, not quite hiding a grimace. "Here's where you're going wrong, Kay. On the purl stitch, where you're bringing the needle in through the front of the loop. You need to bring it in right-to-left. Like this. Then loop the yarn and pull it through, sliding the old stitch off your left-hand needle."

I took my sample from Suzette and repeated her motions,

thrilled to see the loopy stitch on the side facing me.

"You were doing a garter stitch, Kay," Suzette explained. "That's basically knit every row, and it's fine for stuff like washcloths where you want some bulk and you want them to lay flat without having to knit an edge. Knit one row, purl one row alternating gives you a nice flat surface. It's what you see in sweaters and it's the stitch you use in that baby hat pattern."

Suzette lived at the very end of our street, in the oldest house in the neighborhood. It wasn't a Victorian, or Queen Anne style. Her house was a stone-and-log farmhouse that dated back to before the Revolutionary War. Sadly, George Washington had not slept there, and the farmland had been chopped up into the tiny lots and streets that had become this portion of Locust Point. The house still stood, handed down in Suzette's family for eight generations. She'd inherited it from her grandmother two years ago, and instead of selling it and buying a condo in Milford like most single twenty-somethings would have done, Suzette had surprised us all by moving into the place. And by slowly restoring it to the solid beauty it had been when German immigrants built it by hand over two hundred and fifty years ago. She'd even begun working on the split-rail fencing that surrounded the two acres that remained of the original three.

"Think I can try the baby hat pattern now?" I asked, eager to move past washcloths.

Suzette nodded. "This one has a rolled edge instead of ribbed, so it's the easiest. And instead of knitting in the round, you sew up a back seam when you're done." She fingered the crunchy finished end of one of the washcloths with its six knots glued together. "When you're done, I'll show you how to weave in the ends so you don't have this…. this."

I'm sure the newborns would appreciate not having a

bunch of glued knots poking them in the head. "And how about the decrease stitches?"

Suzette hesitated. "If you want to start working on the hat, I can walk you through the decrease stitches as you come to them. Unless you have other plans."

I was a sixty-year-old widow. My only plans tonight included a bottle of Chardonnay on the porch with Daisy. Suzette, on the other hand, was a young woman. "It's a typical Friday night for me, hon. Please stay and join Daisy and me for some wine. And I truly appreciate your helping me with my knitting."

She smiled, her round face creasing in dimples, her soft brown eyes crinkling to narrow slits. "I'd like that. Is Daisy... she's the one with the Wiccan altar in her front yard? The one who put that giant evergreen pentacle on her front door last Christmas?"

That would be Daisy. "Yes. You haven't met her yet? She's a very sweet person. She'll do anything to help someone. One of the nicest, kindest people I know."

Daisy had been a regular at our backyard parties when Eli and I had first moved in. She and I had grown close, but after Eli's accident, I realized how amazing this quirky woman was. When the casseroles and offers to help had died away, when most everyone stopped asking how Eli was, how I was, because the answer was too depressing, Daisy's friendship had never faltered. When all I wanted was to crawl into a hole, to disappear and become nothing but a nursemaid, a caregiver with a hollowed-out dead spot inside, Daisy had dragged me into the light. She'd insisted on coming over and making me do sunrise yoga a few times each week. She'd show up with a bottle of wine or take-out Chinese, or a mushy chick-flick, or some ridiculous game like Hungry Hungry Hippos and for a brief moment, my life wasn't so bleak.

After ten years of helping me survive, when Eli suffered that stroke that had taken his life in a matter of minutes, Daisy had been right there. She'd spent the night so I wouldn't have to be alone. She'd stepped up the sunrise yoga to a daily occurrence. She'd been nearby at the funeral, ready to hand me a tissue, or wrap a comforting arm around my shoulders. For all I cared, the woman could sit on her front porch buck-naked and burn crop circles in her yard. As far as I was concerned, Daisy should be on the fast-track to sainthood.

But she was quirky. And that probably made me love her even more.

Suzette nodded. "Oh, good. I don't know many people in the neighborhood. I've been kinda busy working on Gran's, I mean my, house. I know you, the Sedgewicks, and the Wilsons."

"How about Kat Lars?" I pointed at the woman getting out of her Volvo sedan, dragging a huge briefcase that looked more like overhead-bin luggage than something a person would take to work.

"No. Aren't they the ones opening the bed and breakfast?"

"Yep." I liked Kat. I wasn't so sure I liked her husband, Will, though.

Kat looked up and waved. I motioned her over. She gave us a raised index finger, then took the briefcase inside, trotting over and up my front steps on four-inch navy-blue pumps that matched her smart pantsuit.

"Kat Lars, this is Suzette Hostenfelder. She owns the old farmhouse down at the end of the road."

Kat's dark eyes widened, and she smoothed her dark curly poof of hair back as if she were in the presence of royalty. "Oh my gosh! I *love* that house. I read the husband and wife built it by hand, using logs from the farmland they were clearing. The original house was one room and a loft, and not added onto for the next fifty years. The husband and wife who'd built it raised six kids in that tiny farmhouse. *Six.*"

Suzette glowed, nodded enthusiastically. "My family bought it from their grandchildren. It's a shame we sold all the land off. I've got a picture from just after the Civil War where you can still see the stables and the chicken coop."

"Oh, I'd love to see that." Kat grinned, eyeing one of the chairs on my porch.

"Sit," I told her. "Daisy is coming over in a few and we're all going to have some wine. And Suzette is going to keep me from making a disaster out of my very first baby hat."

Kat plopped down in the chair, looking over at my book with the pattern. "Knitting. I crochet. Mainly I learned so I could make all those lacy doily things for the house so it looked more authentic." She laughed. "I used to make fun of those old-lady houses with the lacy doilies and china wash basins and damask-covered couches, and yet here I am: owner of a three-story Victorian house and suddenly dedicated to making it look like it did a hundred years ago."

"It should add to the appeal of a bed and breakfast," Suzette commented. Then she leaned over my shoulder. "Instead of sliding the needle under one stitch, slide it under two. There. See? It's a decrease, and that type of decrease is typically notated by K2TOG. Do another row and I'll show you the K2PSSO or knit two/pass over decrease."

"I hope so." Kat glanced over at her house. "Will has been so uptight since the downsizing. It's not just the money. He needs this to be a success. He needs to not have one more failure on top of the layoff."

I suddenly felt bad for thinking I didn't really like Will Lars. He was always so high-strung, so tightly wound, so... angry. Maybe he had a reason to be. Maybe he'd mellow out a bit once they started getting regular bookings. I didn't think so.

Daisy waltzed around the huge privet hedges that lined my side porches, the biggest bottle of white wine in her hand that I'd ever seen. It was even frosty.

"Whoa! Glad I bought the gallon-sized," she said, her voice cheerful as she hopped up the steps. Daisy was in blue seersucker capris with a sleeveless white shirt that showed off her tanned arms and jangling, stacked bracelets. I set down my knitting and pulled the tub of plastic wine glasses and silverware from under the table, setting up for our little happy hour party.

"Daisy, this is Suzette Hostenfelder from the old farm down the road. And you know Kat Lars."

The women all smiled at each other, Daisy setting down the wine and wiping her hand on her capris before reaching over the table to shake Suzette's hand. "I knew your grandmother. When I was a kid we used to get in trouble for sneaking onto her property and swimming in the pond. The first few times, your grandfather would come out and chase us off, but eventually they just let us swim. Your grandmother would even bring us out Kool-Aid and cookies on occasion."

Suzette grinned. "He used to yell at us for swimming in it too, although by that time he wasn't able to go past the back porch without taking the riding mower. There's a nasty drop off, and some rocks, and the water is so darned murky that he was always afraid someone would hit their head diving in, or try to swim under a fallen log and get stuck and drown. He was a man who worried about everything, where Gran was a woman who worried about nothing."

Funny how opposites sometimes attracted. I paused my knitting to watch Daisy pour the wine, and thought about Eli and I. We hadn't been opposites. Yes, he'd been a surgeon and I'd been a journalist, but we'd had similar childhoods and had been raised with nearly identical family values. When it came to politics, where to vacation, if we should have beef or chicken for dinner, we agreed more times than not. Then I smiled, thinking of the wine and cigars and movies. I remembered how I'd be wrist-deep in mulch and peat pots, planting out back and drinking some cheap wine cooler while he puffed one of those stinky cigars and drank expensive cognac. But then he'd stub out the cigar, drag me out of the flowerbeds, dirt under my fingernails and hair sticky with sweat to kiss me under the arbor. Maybe Suzette's grandparents had a whole lot more in common than Suzette thought.

"Here." Daisy handed us each a glass and extended hers. "To summer. To cookouts and fireworks. To the town regatta. To family reunions and local carnivals. To playing in the sprinklers and drinking wine on the front porch. To the best neighbors a woman could ask for."

A car door slammed. We all murmured a response to Daisy's inspiring toast, sipped our wine, then looked. It was a man in his forties walking away from his sports car like he was on his way to battle. At the sidewalk, he turned and began to work his way through the maze of mowers and washing machines that were Harry Peter's front lawn.

"Uh oh," Kat breathed, taking a bigger drink of her wine.

"That the nephew?" Daisy asked.

The man had reached the front door in record time and was banging on it with a force that sent the sound clear across the street to us.

"Yes," Kat mumbled into her wine glass. "I think Will called him. I wish he'd just leave that man alone."

Wish Will would leave Mr. Peter's nephew alone? Or leave Mr. Peter alone? Or did Kat wish that the nephew left his uncle alone? I opened my mouth to ask, but shut it because the door across the street had opened and the drama had begun.

For a guy in his eighties, Harry Peter sure had a voice that could carry. I heard enough profanity to make me glad that Judge Beck and his kids weren't home. I also heard the nephew yelling back that his uncle was a crazy old man who wasn't mentally fit to be living on his own.

The gist of the argument seemed to be that the nephew was tired of his uncle's living conditions, that he was sick of dealing with unpaid bills, threatened meter readers and social services workers, and he was fed up with being accused of elder neglect. He followed that up by shouting that if his uncle didn't move into some sort of assisted living with a psych ward, he was going to petition the state to have him committed.

I winced, because I'd done enough articles on the rights of the elderly and the mentally ill over the years that I knew Mr. Peter's nephew's threats lacked teeth. It was near impossible to get a building condemned and someone removed from their home for anything except serious public health and safety threats. It was even more difficult to get someone declared incompetent against their will. They had to pose a clear, significant threat either against themselves or others. And from what I'd seen of Harry Peter's house yesterday, he was just an eccentric man with a dirty house with significant deferred maintenance, a man whose collecting impulses had crossed the line into what might be considered hoarding.

All that the nephew was doing right now was giving the neighborhood a show. And we weren't the only ones watching, either. The Wilsons were trying to pretend they weren't eavesdropping, dead-heading geraniums as if it were a typical activity for a couple to do on a Friday evening. And right next door, leaning over the porch rail and making no attempt to look like he wasn't listening in, was Will Lars.

I turned to his wife, Kat, who was gulping wine like she was a camel in the desert. I was pretty sure if she hadn't had skin the color of mocha, it would now be beet red. Then I looked back over at Will. He was a good-looking man, tall and thin with wavy shoulder-length blond hair pulled back into a man-bun. His hands were in the pockets of his olive-green pants, his tan polo shirt unbuttoned at the neck. He stared at the arguing men dispassionately, then his face twisted into a scowl as he looked at the yard full of appliances.

I didn't really blame him. It was an eyesore. I'd gotten used to staring at it every day, barely even noticed it anymore. But Will Lars seemed unable to look away.

"If he'd just get rid of the junk in the front yard," Kat murmured. "We'd mow the grass for him. We'd pay for some landscaping so it would be pretty and nice. Why does he even have all that stuff? Who needs twelve washing machines, eight dryers, six dishwashers, and twenty lawn mowers?"

"He used to fix them," Daisy said. "When I was a kid, I remember Harry Peter was the go-to guy if you needed something repaired. He used to have a bunch of old ones stacked in his backyard and garage to use as parts. He worked at Himmet Appliance until he retired, but even then, he'd do work on the side."

I hadn't known that. I'd always assumed that the collection in Harry Peter's front yard came from his own house, broken down appliances that he'd replaced but never got around to having hauled away. Or perhaps with the intention of eventually fixing them.

"It's not like he fixes them anymore," Kat replied, her voice with a shrill edge to it.

She loved her husband. And the neighbor's junk-filled yard was driving Will crazy. I understood. But clearly Daisy did not.

"He wants to believe he'll fix them one day," Daisy countered. "He doesn't want to admit that he won't ever be able to do that again, that those machines that were once useful for parts are now only junk. Having them hauled away would be like giving up. It would be like admitting that he was one step closer to death. That's not an easy thing to do, Kat. You should know how hard people cling to what they used to do, what they used to be good at. You should know how difficult it is for people to admit that they'll never be able to return to that thing that once defined them, that once gave them value."

I held my breath, knowing that Daisy was talking about Will. Even so, I still thought of Eli. Even with his cognitive injuries, it had taken years for him to admit to himself that he'd never practice surgery. And it had taken longer for him to resign himself to the fact that he'd never have an alternate career, that he'd be a mostly housebound invalid until he died. The rage and the depression had almost been more than I could bear.

Kat gritted her teeth, then emptied her glass. "Thanks for the wine and conversation, ladies. Have a great weekend."

We watched her practically run down the stairs, speed-walking across the street and climbing to her porch. Once there, she hugged her husband, turning him away from the yard filled with rusted and broken appliances so she could kiss him.

It was the kiss of a woman who desperately loved her husband. It was the kiss of someone who'd do anything to help him, to get him through the darkness he was navigating.

"You dropped a stitch there," Suzette said, breaking the awkward silence. "Let me show you how to pick it up and weave it back into the hat without needing to tear out two rows of stitches."

CHAPTER 4

*W*e made short work of the wine. I was happy-buzzed heading into the house to grab dinner, but I kept thinking of the altercation across the street.

Harry Peter. How long had it been since he'd left his house? I couldn't remember. There were a lot of boxes that got delivered. I assumed food, and anything else he needed. The power company came once a month and if Mr. Peter didn't chase the meter reader off, then the guy weaved his way back to the meter and came back, shaking his head. Whatever maintenance the house had needed, Mr. Peter must have done himself or just left unrepaired.

I hesitated, looking up my winding stairs with the heavy oak handrails. Three stories, then an attic—an attic full of all sorts of junk. Not as much junk as what the guy across the street had, but plenty of things I didn't need. And among them was a really ugly pitcher.

Dinner could wait. I climbed the stair, gasping for breath as the heat hit me the moment I opened the attic door. I'd gone through five boxes before I found the pitcher. At least, I thought it was the pitcher. It had been a gift from Eli's Aunt

Linda. I remember there was a time when I felt the need to prominently display every gift, no matter how much I hated it. I'd come home one day to find that Eli had boxed all the hideous knickknacks up and hauled them up to the attic, telling me life that was too short to stare at ugly vases and candle holders. He was right.

And this pitcher was hideous. It was a glossy cream with alternating bands of navy and burgundy, with gold lacy patterns. Across the center was a series of lavender and pale blue orchids. At least I thought they were orchids.

Aunt Linda was in a nursing home in Milford. She didn't remember the name of her favorite cat. I was pretty sure she didn't remember that she gave us this pitcher for a wedding gift, even if she somehow happened to pop by.

Wrapping it carefully in newspaper, I headed out of the attic and across the street.

It took a while for Mr. Peter to answer my knock, but given the boxes and piles he needed to navigate, I wasn't surprised. There was an odd expression on the man's face when he peeked through the door opening—one part wary, and two parts defeated. The argument with his nephew had taken a lot out of him. Mr. Peter wasn't a young man. Although I'm sure it was exhausting at any age to stand on your front porch and scream at someone.

"Oh. Hello. I thought…"

I smiled and unwrapped the pitcher. "You said you wanted to see this? I figured it would be nice for you to end the evening on a good note."

He caught his breath, his hands reaching toward the pitcher. Then he stopped, yanking his hands back and smiling sheepishly. "Please come inside."

I stepped in, carefully navigating the shelving units with their vases. "Are these new?" I pointed to a set of bone china cat figurines.

"Yes, they are! I just got them yesterday. And look at these." He showed me a series of fish-shaped plates, clearly hand painted. Two had scenic pictures with a woman holding a flower and a milkmaid on them, and the other had...George Washington. I knew it was George Washington because his name was spelled out over his head with the years of his birth and death underneath.

"1945 Quimper. I found these lovelies at an online estate auction and bought the whole set." He motioned to another set of boxes that blocked the path I'd walked to his kitchen just yesterday. How in the world did he get to the back of his house? I looked around and tried to imagine him climbing over boxes, shelves, and stacked items like a child on a playground, and just couldn't see it.

He took the pitcher with far more reverence than I'd ever handled it. "Oh, this is truly exquisite." He turned it over. "See, here's the mark with the swoosh underneath and the three crowns. Rorstrand started making pottery in the late eighteenth century in Stockholm, Sweden. The three-crown mark has been in use since 1884. This English style of porcelain was in production in the late nineteenth century. This is a lovely piece, obviously well taken care of. You could probably get between three and four hundred for it, and I'm sure collectors would be eager to snatch this beauty up."

I had a feeling that the reason it was so well preserved was that it had been owned by people who felt it was too ugly to take out of the attic, let alone actually use. But it was the fact that a pitcher that had spent the last fifteen years stuffed in a box in my attic was worth hundreds of dollars that amazed me. This little visit was like an episode of Antiques Roadshow. Three hundred dollars. Or possibly four hundred dollars.

Huh. Maybe Aunt Linda didn't hate us after all.

He handed it back. "Swansons in Milford might buy it off

you. They carry a lot of estate pieces, although they tend to specialize in paintings and furniture."

I got the idea he was hoping I'd give it to him from the longing in his face as I took the pitcher. Sorry, buddy. This thing is going to pay for my hot tub repair.

"How do you know so much about pottery and china?" I asked to fill the awkward I'm-not-giving-you-the-ugly-pitcher silence.

He smiled, picking up a plate from on top of a book and wiping the dust from it with his hand. "When I was little, my grandmother loved china. She had three sets and rotated use of them depending on the season. I'd stand in front of her china cabinet and stare at the patterns. Her end tables had little figurines and crystal knickknacks on lace doilies. The bookshelves had bisque animals, glossy cherub angels, little painted metal pugs, but it was the china that had fascinated me. She'd had these special collector's plates mounted on the walls where most people would have pictures. In a way, they *were* her pictures—blue Delft scenes of Holland, little girls with curled hair, sitting on a stool reading while a fluffy dog curled at her feet, detailed flowers with gold foil accents covering the entire surface of the front of the plate. All that meant 'Grandma' to me, so when she died, that's what I kept from her estate."

I understood the sentimental value of things, how they linked to memories and invoked a visceral emotional response, but Mr. Peter clearly had a lot more china in his house than his grandmother's collection. "When did memories of your Grandma grow into a...collecting hobby?"

It seemed rude to call it hoarding to his face, although clearly this had long gone beyond collecting.

"Once I got Grandma's plates out of the holders and got to look at the back, I got curious, so I started researching what the marks meant, what years the plates had been manufactured. Then I'd think about what was happening that year in history and imagine my grandmother, or anyone actually, in that period of time. I started buying plates similar to Grandma's, feeling like I was dipping my toe in a little bit of history each time I held one. Then I started buying depression-era glassware, then Faience. For a while I bought silverware. I've got a box over here with a twelve-piece set of rose-patterned Stieff. I've even got all the serving pieces—pickle forks, mustard knives, and all."

It was an enchanting story, pulling at the journalist side of me. What an amazing lifestyle article this would make. But clearly there was somewhere this had all gone wrong, where Mr. Peter's nostalgic collection of china and dinnerware had turned into musty boxes and a house that resembled an overstuffed storage unit. And none of this explained the yard full of rusted washing machines.

"I heard you were an appliance repairman before you retired," I commented. "Do you still work on stuff on the side?"

Mr. Peter's face fell. "I want to. I try, but it's hard to get parts anymore, and the arthritis in my hands and back makes it difficult for me to work on anything. Small engines and major appliances were my specialty, my career. I used to fix things like stoves and washing machines, window air conditioners, and lawn mowers. That was back when people didn't just throw things away every time they broke. Appliances were expensive. It was like buying a car. You fixed them when they broke and wanted them to last your whole life."

I thought of all the old washing machines in his front yard and remembered how my mother had kept her stove for nearly forty years. She'd had elements replaced, but beyond that, the thing had always worked reliably. Yeah, it looked old and dated, and there was a place where the enamel had chipped from dropping a wrench on it. She'd gone to Sears and bought a little bottle of paint to cover the chip, but had picked up the wrong shade, so there had been a dark blob of paint on a sea of lighter avocado green. When she'd died and we'd had some charity haul it off, it had still worked.

"It's a shame," I commented. "Retro appliances are really in fashion right now. I'm sure the real thing, fixed up and working, would fetch a good bit of money."

His eyes lit up. "I've got three fifties-era stoves in the backyard. Maybe I could use one for parts, order what else I need, and get two of them running. Do you think someone would want them?"

My heart twisted. It wasn't the money. Mr. Peter clearly had enough money if he was buying truckloads of china from estate sales. He wanted to be useful, to be remembered, to be seen. If an old plate kept his grandmother alive in his memory, if a set of silverware harkened back to a history that shouldn't be forgotten, then maybe he'd be remembered, too. If stoves that had been thrown away as old, as no longer useful, could be loved and cherished once more, then maybe the same could be true of him. Then I looked down and saw his thin fingers with their big swollen knuckles, saw how he leaned on a box for support, wheezing with each breath, and realized that there was no way Mr. Peter was going to be able to fix up old stoves in the back yard.

But neither of us had to acknowledge that. A little bit of fantasy went a long way toward soothing a ragged soul. "That's a wonderful idea, Mr. Peter!" I exclaimed. "I'm sure you've got lots of treasurers here that with the turn of a screw could be useful once more. Personally, I'd love it if you had an old-style toaster, one where the sides opened up?"

He grinned, his eyes crinkling with deep lines at the corners. "I do have some of those toasters. As I recall, they're upstairs in one of the back bedrooms with the mixers."

"Oh, I'd love a mixer too," I told him. So much for selling

this pitcher and using it to pay for the hot tub repair. It seems instead I was going to be buying refurbished appliances that I didn't need from my eccentric neighbor. It would be worth it to see the happiness on the man's face.

"Absolutely, Mrs. Carrera. Come by next week and I should have one, or maybe both, ready for you." He escorted me through the winding pathways of his living room to the front door. "You have a good evening, now. And take care of that beautiful pitcher."

Oh, I intended to. And first chance I got, this pitcher was going straight to Swanson's in Milford.

CHAPTER 5

I made my way back across the street, squeezing through my doorway while clutching the pitcher in my arms and trying to keep Taco from slipping out the door with my foot. I managed to get myself in and the door closed with the cat on the right side of it. In response, he plopped his butt down, stared up at my face, and meowed repeatedly at me.

"No. You keep going over to Mr. Peter's house and he's feeding you, so inside you stay until you lose some weight."

Meow.

Because Taco knew if he persisted, he'd most likely wear me down and I'd end up letting him out. Maybe I could at night, when Mr. Peter would be asleep and less likely to feed him? But I liked having my cat safely in the house at night, curled up on the end of my bed. No, I'd just worry if he was out all night.

I set the pitcher on the dining room table, then went into the kitchen to contemplate dinner options. It was getting kind of late to cook anything requiring prep work or a lengthy time in the oven, so I ended up just making a big sandwich with some iced tea to counteract the happy-hour porch wine I'd had earlier.

Taco's I-want-to-go-outside meows turned into I-want-some-of-your-sandwich meows. I ignored him and he finally gave up, heading upstairs in a huff. I hoped he wasn't the sort of cat who'd take revenge on me by clawing up one of my plants or pooping on the floor. If he was going to be more of an indoor cat than an outdoor cat, I'd need to invest in additional cat toys. Cat enrichment devices. Maybe there was something I could make? I had some carpet scraps up in the attic. Actually, I had a lot of stuff up in the attic. One of the downfalls of owning a large house was that a person tended to fill the space and not be as diligent about getting rid of things. It was easier to just throw stuff up in the attic or haul it off to a charity then think about whether I really wanted it or not. I was far from living like Mr. Peter, but there were a lot of things that probably needed to go. And perhaps some of them, like this pitcher, could yield some much-needed money.

I ate my sandwich at the dining room table, looking at the ugly pitcher and trying to remember all the stuff up in the attic. Crystal I didn't need. That holiday-themed dish set. The beads and wire and tools I'd bought ages ago when I thought I might want to make jewelry and sell it. Baskets I'd kept because they were handy to put banana nut bread in when I was giving baked goods as Christmas gifts. And speaking of which—all that Christmas wrapping paper I'd bought from local kids before I realized it was so much easier to use gift bags and tissue paper.

That wasn't all. There were a lot of Eli's things that I probably needed to go through. I'd boxed up and donated his clothes the month after the funeral. There was no reason for me to keep them, but even that had been hard. There were the clothes that Eli had worn the last ten years of his life, but

I'd also had an entire closet upstairs of his pre-accident clothes. There were the suits, the dress shirts, pants, and bow ties that he'd worn each day to the hospital. There were his scrubs, the emblematic white "doctor" coats that he wore over his dress clothes when not in surgery. I'd kept them in the closet after the accident, not wanting at first to accept that my husband was never going to be that surgeon again. It seemed wrong to pack them away at that time, like I was giving up on him, like I didn't have faith that he'd pull through this and after some rehab, after both physical and cognitive therapy, he'd be able to return to work once more.

Then as months stretched into years, I'd kept them in the closet for another reason. The Eli downstairs wasn't the man I'd married. He wasn't the man I'd fallen in love with when I was an English major in college. He was somebody else, and if I packed away the earlier Eli's clothes, I'd be not only admitting that, but I'd be letting go of those little bits of my— of *our*—life before the accident took it all away. I kept those clothes, holding onto them just as I held onto the hope that one day, someday, he'd be that person again. I couldn't be the one to smash those dreams, to take away the chance that he'd once more be Dr. Carrera, because I, too, was living that fantasy.

A decade he'd lived like that after the accident. Even on the day before the stroke took him from me forever, even though I knew in my mind that he'd never be the old Eli again, I'd still held hope. I'd still, deep in my heart, had a tiny glimmer of faith. I'd still kept those clothes in our closet.

It took weeks after his death for me to box them up and send them away. I'd packed up all his other belongings. I'd already sent his other clothes to charity. Those trappings of the surgeon he'd been were the last to go.

After I'd finished my sandwich, I poured a measured amount of Happy Cat into Taco's bowl, and while he was scarfing it down, I snuck up to the attic. In an hour, I'd carted down a few boxes of things I felt might be of interest to Swanson's. The rest could wait for another day. The whole exercise made me feel empathy for Mr. Peter because one hour of deciding what could go and what should stay was exhausting. If my house had been at all like his, I would have found the whole thing overwhelming.

It was close to ten o'clock when Judge Beck arrived home with the kids. Madison was still wearing her softball uniform, half-dragging a backpack that looked like it weighed fifty pounds. Henry was more energetic, and I remembered that he'd only had practice tonight, while his sister had a game. Tomorrow that was reversed, with Madison's practice early, and Henry's game later. The kids headed upstairs with quick 'good nights', but Judge Beck went back out to his car and returned with a box, which he proceeded to unpack on my dining room table. Folder after folder came out of the box, as if it were one of those containers magicians use to produce an endless stream of colorful scarves.

"Feel free to use the desk in the study," I told him. Not that I cared whether he worked at the dining room table. I simply thought he might get more privacy in the study.

"There's no desk in the universe big enough to hold all this." More folders appeared from the box. "I'm not even sure your dining room table is big enough. I may need to use the floor space."

Yikes. "Can I help? Is there anything I can do?"

"Clone me? I'm just grateful I don't have court on the weekends or I'd be in big trouble."

"My cloning devices are all on the fritz right now, but I can offer you a sandwich, or put on a pot of coffee."

He looked up, a tired smile on his face. "Coffee would be lovely. We ate at the game, although I'm not sure I can call microwaved hotdogs or those little square frozen pizzas to be food."

"Snob," I called back to him as I headed to the kitchen. Within minutes the coffee was percolating, sending its intoxicating aromas throughout the lower floor of the house. I waited until the pot was half full, then paused it to pour the judge a cup. "What do you take in it? I can't remember."

"Just a spoonful of sugar, please."

Helps the medicine go down? Helps the briefs and summaries read easier? I stirred in a spoonful of sugar and carried the cup out to the dining room to see Judge Beck, folder poised in mid-air as he stared at the object on my table.

"What in the world is this ugly—I mean, this…this."

He must be exhausted to have been jolted out of his normal calm poise by a piece of china.

"You mean that hideous thing? Why, it's a nineteenth-century Rorstrand pitcher which, I'm informed, is worth anywhere between three and four hundred dollars."

The judge's mouth dropped open, folder still hovering a foot above the table's surface. "You're joking."

"No, I am not. Eli's Aunt Linda gave it to us for our wedding and after suffering through five years of having it displayed in our front window, we packed it up in the attic. I'm going through a bunch of things up there, clearing out what I don't want. Fortunately, I don't want that, and it's worth money, so win-win."

"And what will you do with your newfound riches?"

Pay for the hot tub repairs. "Buy a toaster. And a mixer."

He blinked, finally lowering the folder to the table. "I used the toaster this morning. It's fine. And I don't recall you saying there was anything wrong with the mixer."

"Oh, both appliances are still working perfectly," I told him blithely. "But Mr. Peter from across the street does antique appliance restoration and he has one of those side-opening toasters and a mixer from the fifties that he's going to sell me."

Judge Beck stared at me. "Who are you and what have you done with my landlady? Are you Kay's evil twin? An alien who has assumed her likeness in order to replace our perfectly good modern appliances with heavy, less-functional and far more expensive antique ones?"

"I'm still Kay. I'm just a sucker with a soft heart," I told him. "I've lived here for over thirty years and I've never really talked to the guy across the street until yesterday."

His eyebrows shot up. "How did you make the leap from 'talking to' to 'buying a bunch of crap from'?"

I raised my hands. "I don't know. He was telling me about his grandmother's china collection, and how he used to repair appliances for a living, and next thing I knew I was committing to buy a toaster from him. And he looked so darned happy that next thing I knew, I was buying a mixer, too."

Judge Beck looked down into the box and pulled another folder out. "Now that I know your weakness, I'll be sure to keep all the Girl Scouts from your door. And those college kids selling knife sets."

I remembered all the wrapping paper in the attic and thought that perhaps he wasn't too far off in his estimation of my ability to resist an emotion-based sales pitch. Or lack thereof.

"See if I ever share my Thin Mints with you, Buster." I grabbed my laptop out of my bag. "I'm heading up. Turn off the coffee pot when you're done?"

He nodded, and I left him, still pulling folders from the box, to go upstairs to my room. Ten o'clock was a bit early for me to retire, but with the judge ensconced in my dining room, I felt the need to curl up in my pajamas, under the covers, and check a few things on my laptop, maybe even watch some cat videos. As if he read my thoughts, Taco raced past me on the stairs, tearing at full speed into my room and leaping on the bed so he was sure to score his favored spot.

I got ready for bed and crawled under the covers, feeling incredibly content. Taco moved up to my side, butting his head against my arm. I petted him, opening up my laptop one-handed and typing a few things into the search engine.

According to the wisdom of the internet, it was very difficult to force someone out of their home and into assisted living. It seemed that it took a judge's order, and that the law was reluctant to take away an individual's right to live as they so chose unless they posed a danger to themselves or to others. And that was danger as in a fear of grievous harm or death. An aunt with mobility issues couldn't be forced out of her home because her family was afraid that she was going to fall down her stairs, even if she'd done so before. It would take continuous falls within a short window of time, in which she'd been unable to contact anyone for help for an unacceptable amount of time to even give a judge a moment's pause. There needed to be a pattern, a repetition of behavior. Anyone could accidently leave a pot on the stove and cause a minor fire, but that, plus flooding the basement, plus backing the car through the garage door, plus forgetting medication, plus not showering for two weeks might, and I mean might, rise to the level of involuntary commitment. Based on what I'd seen of Mr. Peter, this would not be a course of action that would yield the nephew's desired results.

As for Will Lars, I didn't think he had any better chance of getting the house condemned or Mr. Peter evicted. If my neighbor had been renting, it might have been easier as a landlord would be able to show violation of the lease, or just end the lease at the end of the term under pressure from neighborhood complaints. But since Mr. Peter owned the property and had for longer than I'd lived here, the only way to get him out would be structural issues in the property that created an unsafe place to live either for him, or for the adjacent properties. And that just wasn't the case. As I'd told J.T., the city officials were likely to cite him on a few codes, then drag out enforcement forever. The worst I could see was the narrow passages which would make it difficult for the fire department to attempt a rescue, or to get control of any sort of blaze. In my experience, the city would issue a list of basic improvements, Mr. Peter would eventually perform them, then all would be fine. And there would still be washing machines in the front lawn and stacks of boxes and dinnerware strewn throughout the house.

At midnight, I snapped the laptop shut and yawned, sitting it on the bedside table. There was a cold drafty area on that side of the bed, and out of the corner of my eye I saw that old familiar shadow; only this time he sat on the edge of the bed, as if he wasn't sure if he was welcome or not.

"I'm going to sleep," I told the shadow. "Don't wake Taco, and don't put your cold feet on me."

I turned off the light, not sure if the shadow stayed or left, if he climbed in beside me or continued to perch on the edge of the bed. He *wasn't* welcome under the covers. Nobody was. It had been ten years since someone had shared my bed, and right now, I couldn't bear the thought of anyone but Taco curled up in the blankets with me.

CHAPTER 6

I came downstairs Saturday morning to find all the folders back in the box, which was now in a corner beside the dining room table. The smell of coffee filled the air, and when I walked into the kitchen I saw a box of donuts on the island counter. From the thumping noises over my head, the kids were up and running around.

Practice. Game. Judge Beck had stashed a few cases of soda in the kitchen to throw into a cooler for the kids, and a note on the fridge told me he'd already arranged for pizza delivery, and that several bags of chips were in the pantry. I stole a cruller from the donut box and started pulling ingredients out of the cabinet, prepping to make a cake. If I hustled, it could be cooling on the counter by the time I left for my ten o'clock ophthalmologist appointment.

Although cooling anything on the counter probably wasn't a good idea, I thought as Taco sat at my feet meowing insistently. I couldn't let him outside, and the moment those cakes were unattended, he'd be up on the counter, stuffing his whiskered little face.

Hmmm. I couldn't cool them in the fridge, or in the still-hot oven. Maybe I could throw some tea towels over them and put them in the wine cellar downstairs. It had a door to keep Taco out. I'd just have to remember that I'd put them there in time for the party. It would be frustrating to go through all this effort only to discover hard, moldy cakes in the wine cellar two weeks from now.

I was taking stock of my ingredients when a herd of elephants came down the stairs.

"I want to feed Taco!" Madison announced, skidding into the kitchen and flipping the lid open on the donut box. "Hey, who ate one?"

"I did. Landlord tax," I told her. "And it's Henry's turn to feed Taco."

The boy reached over his sister's shoulder, grabbing a glazed with chocolate icing and sprinkles and sticking his tongue out at his sister.

"Mature," she commented, taking a Boston cream.

Henry stuffed the donut in his mouth and held it there as he pulled out the Happy Cat and carefully measured the amount for Taco's breakfast as the cat pounced on the bowl. Henry was much better at following Taco's dietary restrictions, where Madison tended to top off the measuring cup a bit. The cat had his head in the bowl before Henry was done pouring.

"What kind of cake do you and the girls want for tonight?" I asked Madison.

She eyed the ingredients on the counter. "Nothing too melty. A pound cake maybe? Can we use those cranberries in the freezer?"

The ones I liked to plop in my wine? Not that Madison knew about that. I'd expected a request for chocolate, chocolate, and more chocolate. "Really? Cranberry pound cake?"

She nodded, swiping the custard out of the center of her

donut with a finger. "I like pound cakes. And I like cranberries."

I got to thinking. "Cranberry orange? I can make a vanilla glaze to give it a bit of sweetness."

"And walnuts? For some crunch?"

An idea was stirring in my mind, and it didn't have much to do with tonight's party. "Do you like to cook, Madison?"

She laughed. "I burn water. I'd rather buy takeout than cook, but I always like baking cookies at Christmas time, and I like to make cakes. I've always used the box mixes, though."

"There are some good box cakes out there," I told her, "but if you want, we can have a cake baking day sometime soon. I've got lots of recipe books, including a bunch from when I was a kid. We'll pick something out and I'll supervise while you make it."

She grinned, the chocolate on her mouth making her seem younger than fifteen. "Dad's birthday is in June. I want to make him a birthday cake."

Perfect. "You start looking at recipes, pick one out, and write down the ingredients that we need. I'm sure your dad would love it."

"Love what?" Judge Beck walked in and eyed the donut box. "Hey, who ate my cruller?"

Oops.

"Never mind." He grabbed the box in one hand and a go-cup of coffee with the other. "We've got to roll or we'll be late. Henry, is your stuff loaded in the car?"

"Yep!"

"Madison?"

The girl sighed. "For the millionth time, yes. Bye, Miss Kay. Thank you!"

I waved the three of them off, shouting a quick warning not to let Taco slip out the door, then went back to my ingredients. Walnuts. An orange. Cranberries. Flour. Salt, baking

49

powder, sugar, butter, eggs, and milk. Vanilla extract. I tapped a finger to my lip, then looked around to make sure the judge and the kids were gone before I pulled a little bottle of Grand Marnier out of the cabinet. The alcohol would cook off, and it would give the pound cake an added orangey flavor.

Honestly, this wasn't much more trouble than a box cake, and it would taste a whole lot better. I peeled and zested the orange, then stuck the sections in a saucepan to boil. Once they were cooking, I chopped the nuts and added cranberries to the cooking orange sections. Then I beat the butter and sugar, adding the eggs, booze, and vanilla when it was smooth and creamy. That done, I added flour and milk, alternating while the mixer worked its magic. Then I folded in the cooked fruit and chopped nuts and poured the batter into a greased and floured pan. While the pound cake cooked, I got my shower and dressed, then pulled it from the oven and barricaded it from the cat to let it cool for ten minutes. Just before I needed to leave, I inverted it onto a wire rack and draped a clean tea towel over it, carrying it down to the wine cellar to finish cooling.

Taco followed me, determined to orchestrate a trip-and-fall that would result in the cake on the floor and in his belly, but I managed to foil his plans and get it safely out of cat-reach to cool.

Next, there was a battle at the door to squeeze through without the cat escaping. Once outside, I was home free and on my way to the eye doctor, actually excited about this evening's activities. Teenage girls. Pizza and chips. Soda and cake. Hot tub and lots of giggles and, no doubt, conversations about boys and school, college, and softball.

How my life had changed in just three months. And I was loving every minute of it.

CHAPTER 7

"*T*here's nothing wrong, Kay." Dr. Berkowitz wheeled his chair back and regarded me somberly. Today he had on a shirt with Yoda on the front. "You do have floaters", he told me. "I can see the viscous fluid. They're not to a level where I'd want to risk any sort of procedure to try to clear them."

He said this at each appointment. While I was relieved there wasn't anything wrong with my eyesight, the other explanation wasn't particularly comforting. I might have floaters, but the shadows weren't anything like what the doctor had described. They looked and acted more like blurry, dark gray spirits. So what I was seeing wasn't an ocular problem, it was a mental one. Or a paranormal one.

"Dr. Berkowitz, do you believe in ghosts?" My next course of action might be to make an appointment for psychiatric counseling, but I felt the need to confide in someone who might have a different take on what I'd been experiencing.

He eyed me with surprise. "Ghosts? Not really. I think sometimes we do feel a presence, but I'm not sure if that's

51

our minds trying to soothe us after a loss, or if a loved one truly stays behind to help ease us into life without them. But the haunted houses and all that? I truly believe those are just imaginations running wild."

I took a deep breath, steeling myself to admit something truly embarrassing. "These things I'm seeing aren't floaters as you're describing them. If there's nothing wrong with my eyes, then these shadows are ghosts. There's one that is around me every evening, and occasionally during the day, just walking beside me, or standing nearby. I can see him just out of the corner of my eye."

The doctor tilted his head, his face full of sympathy as he patted my shoulder. "Kay, you've lost your husband, the man you were with for nearly forty years. When someone is by your side for that long, I believe it's normal for your mind to imagine him still there, nearby and doing the things he always did."

Maybe. And the shadow *had* become a comforting presence. But I didn't want to think that my grief was holding Eli's spirit here, or that his guilt over leaving me kept him from his afterlife. Maybe instead of a psychiatrist, I needed to go see Reverend Lincoln. Or join that grief group at the Baptist church.

But it wasn't just the evening ghost, the one that might be Eli, that I was seeing. I remembered the day I'd found Caryn Swanson's body. I'd seen that shadow twice, and it had clearly been a different sort of experience than what I had when I was visited by my evening friend.

"What if it's not just grief?" I mused. "One of those shadows showed me where Caryn Swanson's body was."

He patted my shoulder again, but now his expression was full of discomfort, as if he wanted to change the conversation back to medical stuff, or the weather. "*That* was probably a floater. It's most likely a combination of floaters and your imagination due to grief. Maybe you should talk to someone."

He was right. And it was becoming clear that my ophthalmologist wasn't the person I needed to seek help from in this issue. I thanked Dr. Berkowitz and headed out, swinging by the Farmer's Market for fresh strawberries, then by a craft store to peruse their yarn selection. I hadn't worked on the hat last night after our porch happy hour, but I'd have some time this afternoon, and I was determined to complete the project. My learn-to-knit kit had held enough yarn to make one baby hat, a scarf, and three washcloths. Admittedly, I'd made nine washcloths over the last three months because I'd needed to disassemble quite a few of them, including my first attempt which unraveled when I'd attempted to clean a dish with it. The scarf…well, the scarf wasn't exactly the sort of thing that I wanted to wear in public. I was seriously considering tearing it apart and starting it over now that I'd learned a bit more about shaping and stitches.

New yarn would energize me. It would jumpstart my creativity and rekindle the enthusiasm I'd had when I first bought the kit. Knitting the same thing over and over was tedious enough without having to use the exact same yarn for every project.

Once inside, I lost myself in bulky single-ply, silky lace-weight, and fanciful yarn that had fuzzies and specks and something that resembled bird feathers. I walked out with a bag full of new yarns, not quite sure if I'd be able to use any of them to make either washcloths or baby hats. Although the bird-feather one would make a truly interesting scarf. How eccentric I'd look strutting around this fall sporting something that looked like a flamboyant turquoise boa.

Once home, I had a wonderful afternoon, drizzling the vanilla glaze over the pound cake, finishing the baby hat, which actually did look like a baby hat, and watching a movie

I'd recorded. An hour before Judge Beck was due to drop Madison and the girls off, I went back to the attic and dug up the old Christmas lights, hauling them outside to string around trees, the gazebo, the hot tub, and the fence.

There'd been a time when these lights had surrounded every window and gable of our house. They'd stretched across the roofline, winding around the porch railing, outlining our house in tiny white dots every night from the day after Thanksgiving until New Years'. The first year Eli had attempted to hang them himself, quickly realizing that a surgeon probably shouldn't be perched up on a ladder, trying to clip strands of lights onto the edge of the roof. I'd been so relieved when after the first strand had gone up, he'd admitted defeat and hired the guy who'd done our roof to take it on as a side job.

They'd been up when Eli had his accident, just two days before New Year's Eve. And although Ralph had come by on January second to take them down, I'd told him not to. I'd always found it depressing to see our house shadowed and dark, the only illumination the porch light and the lamp in the bay window. I hated when we took the lights down, as if we were admitting defeat against the darkness of winter, giving in to the inevitable death that the cold nights of January symbolized. Going back and forth each day to the hospital, I'd watch over my husband who'd been so vibrant, so intelligent and alive just days before, and wonder if he would ever come out of the coma, if he'd live to see spring. When I'd pull in my driveway in the dark of night, feeling the icy fingers of winter wrap around me, the only thing that symbolized hope was those Christmas lights.

The symbolism of death in removing the lights each year was easier to face with Eli by my side. That year I refused. And when the ambulance brought him home, and my husband was safely ensconced in the former study in a hospital bed, I asked Ralph to come by and take them down. I no longer needed those lights because Eli was home, and with hard work and time, he'd fully recover. I fully believed that by the time Ralph put those Christmas lights up again, Eli would be walking, driving to the hospital each day, telling me about his patients and what surgeries he had that week. I no longer needed those lights, because everything was going to be okay. I'd beat back the darkness. We'd fought death and won. The rest would be a piece of cake.

The Christmas lights never went up again. And I quickly learned that you can fight death, but you never really win.

The kids arrived at the same time as the pizza delivery man. They poured from Judge Beck's SUV like jumping beans, hopping across the lawn, squealing and laughing and carrying little drawstring bags. I signed for the pizza and waved as an exhausted looking Judge Beck and a relieved Henry pulled away from the curb, heading to the next round of teenage sports.

This pool party had been the easiest, most pleasant party I'd ever hosted. Madison's friends were polite and courteous. After devouring pizza, chips, and soda, they helped clean up, then went inside to change, tearing out in a whirlwind of bikinis and long hair to climb into the hot tub. The sun was going down, so I flicked the lights on and was thrilled with their exclamations about how magical it all was.

When I went in to get the cake, I realized that something was missing… Or rather, *someone* was missing. Taco. I'd fed him his dinner, and rather than lock him in the basement, I'd warned the girls about keeping him in the house. I didn't blame them. He was a sneaky cat, and I'd known it was a matter of time before he slipped between someone's legs and dashed to freedom.

Darn it all. No doubt he was over at Mr. Peter's house eating chicken sandwiches. Luckily, he was a cat who liked his routine, and he'd be back in an hour or so, before I headed up to bed.

A bit after sunset, several cars pulled up to the curb and I realized that Madison's guests' parents had arrived to pick them up. Actually, it was three mothers who were walking up my porch steps, and they were an hour early. I answered the door and introduced myself, thankful that I'd made a large pound cake. Then I shuffled them into the back yard while I put coffee on and grabbed extra plates and forks.

It wasn't until I'd gone outside that I realized that the three women were especially well coiffed for a Saturday evening. Had there been some sort of charity function, or Toastmaster's meeting or something? Or perhaps mothers of teenage girls always dressed in skinny jeans and snug, low-cut tops with makeup and glossy, straightened hair on Saturdays. Although I didn't remember Heather, Madison and Henry's mother, ever looking like this when she'd come by on the weekends to pick up the kids.

The girls and women alike loved the cranberry, orange, walnut pound cake, and I gave Madison credit for the idea. The girls got dressed, spent a few moments looking for Taco, then one by one, they headed off, all thanking me politely and telling Madison they'd see her on Monday.

I was surprised when I felt an arm reach around my waist to give me a quick hug. "Thank you, Miss Kay. You're the best."

"You're welcome, hon." I hugged Madison back. "This was fun. Your friends are very nice. They're welcome over any time, as long as your dad says it's okay. I want to have a neighborhood barbeque soon, so maybe you can invite one or two of them over. There aren't many girls your age on this street."

"That would be fun." She turned to leave, then hesitated at the doorway, spinning around to shoot me a dazzling smile.

"I'm glad Dad decided to live here. I mean, I wish he and Mom would have stayed together, but they fought all the time and it felt like the South Pole every time they were in a room together. They don't seem any happier apart, but Dad spends more time with us now, and we got to meet you and kind of adopt Taco. I love your house, and your cat, and I know we have a lot more fun here then we would have had if Dad had rented an apartment somewhere."

I blinked back tears. "I'm glad your Dad moved here, too. I really like having you three around, and so does Taco. Speaking of which, I need to go find my cat. Can you clean up the rest of the cake and coffee, and turn off the light strands when you're done?"

"Sure thing, Miss Kay." She skipped up the steps and a few seconds later I heard the back door slam.

Turning around, I steeled myself for what I needed to do. It was only nine o'clock. Both the porch light and several indoor lights were on at Mr. Peter's house. It was time for me to retrieve my cat before he had a chance to eat the poor guy out of house and home. Straightening my shirt, I took a deep breath and headed across the street, weaving my way through the old appliances as I made my way to the front door.

I knocked, then waited, remembering how long it took Mr. Peter to make his way to the front of the house. After a few minutes, I was starting to feel like an idiot, standing on this guy's porch. Thinking that maybe he hadn't heard me the first time, I knocked again. And again.

This time I heard something, but it wasn't the door being unlocked or footsteps, it was a cat meowing.

"Taco? Mr. Peter?"

The meowing got louder. I tried to peek in the side window, hoping to see my cat, but all I saw was boxes, storage tubs, the back of a filthy sofa, and light somehow filtering through the gaps in all the junk. "Mr. Peter? Are you okay? I'm so sorry to disturb you, but I'm here to get my cat."

I still heard nothing. Well, nothing except for my cat. He was probably upstairs or at the back of the house. There was no doorbell, and with all the junk in his house, it was probably difficult to hear me knocking. My mind automatically imagined the worst, that he'd had a medical emergency or fallen and couldn't get up. Did Mr. Peter have one of those emergency button thingies? I hadn't recalled seeing one. Worried, and figuring that he must have been okay an hour ago to let my cat inside his house, I turned the doorknob and found it unlocked.

"Mr. Peter?" I called into the house. A cat ran to me with a chirping noise, fur fluffed out in alarm. It was Taco. It had to be Taco, but what in the world had he gotten into? The fur that wasn't standing on end was wet, the light parts of his gray stripes dark. I opened the door further and bent down to scoop him up, smelling a metallic scent just as my hands felt his sticky wet fur and my eyes registered the red paw prints on the floor.

"Mr. Peter?" There was a high-pitched urgency to my voice as I put Taco down and went into the room. He'd fallen. He'd fallen and hit his head on something, and that's was why he hadn't answered the door. The only thing that kept me from dialing 911 was my irrational thought that Taco had broken a bottle of old raspberry syrup and had rolled in it. It would be so embarrassing if emergency services came screaming down the street only to find Mr. Peter in the shower.

"Hello?" It was more difficult to get through the room than it had been before. Boxes were blocking what had been the pathway, and everything had been shifted so that I had to navigate my way as if I were traversing switchbacks on a mountain climb. When I managed to get past what had once been a living room, I realized that Mr. Peter was probably not in the shower. He was a hoarder, but a reasonably organized one. The boxes knocked onto their sides, broken dishes, and smashed kitchen appliances sent my fears into overdrive. Had he suffered a heart attack and crashed into his belongings in a desperate attempt to get to the phone?

Climbing over a dusty dresser, I saw a pair of legs on the kitchen floor. It took me a while to push the boxes away, and find Mr. Peter facedown in a pool of what clearly was his own blood. He wasn't moving. And next to him, jabbed point first into a brown cardboard box, was a sword.

CHAPTER 8

$\mathcal{I}$n reality, it took the police less than five minutes to arrive, but to my mind, it felt like hours. Unable to stand there and stare at my neighbor without making some attempt to help, or at least check his vitals, I went to him, squatted down, and put a hand on his back.

"Mr. Peter?" I asked softly. I couldn't feel him breathing, and when I picked up his hand, I couldn't feel anything but what I was positive was my own racing pulse. Wanting to make sure, I attempted to turn him over without success. It was like trying to move five bags of sand that were attached together at the corners. All I managed to do was get blood on my hands and arms.

Clearly not able to provide any sort of medical attention and unwilling to contaminate what was obviously a crime scene, I stood back and waited, holding my hands awkwardly away from my body so as to not get blood on my pants or shirt.

I was numb, filled with horror that was squashed between a combination of practicality and a macabre sense of humor. I'd gone my whole life without seeing a dead body... Now I'd seen two in the last three months, not counting Eli, who had technically died enroute to the hospital. My second murder. Well, I assumed it was a murder. I eyed the sword and began to think of all the strange accident scenarios whereupon an elderly man was stabbed by a museum-quality replica in his house. If he fell at just the right angle, maybe the sword could bounce off the floor and launch itself into the side of a box. Or maybe Mr. Peter had gotten some devastating news either about his health or about the authenticity of a beloved piece of china and had committed seppuku, only to ram the sword into a box after committing the act. Or Taco had startled him while he was cutting tomatoes with the sword and he'd impaled himself, then thrown the sword into the box in anger before succumbing to his injuries.

What made the whole thing worse was a shadow that had appeared just out of my line of sight, over toward the stove. It hovered, then moved toward the body, looking for a moment as if it had crouched down, then rose to drift over toward the sword in the box.

I hoped the ghost didn't have poltergeist abilities, because I doubted the police would believe my story of a specter that contaminated the crime scene and disturbed evidence in a homicide investigation. And I fully believed that this was a ghost. It didn't have the same feel as the ghost that kept me company in the evenings, and its shape wasn't the same. If I believed in ghosts, then it would be logical to assume that this was Mr. Peter's spirit remaining behind after his violent demise. His, or its, presence made me just as panicked as the blood on my hands. The man had seemed to like me, and he definitely liked my cat, but who knew what a ghost of a murdered man might do?

I was grateful the police showed up when they did, before I had the chance to explore any further wild flights of imagination. I was pulled through yet another maze into what seemed to have been a dining room at one point, and questioned while the police gawked at the degree of clutter and waited for the M.E. and techs to arrive. The ghost followed me, hovering over a dust-covered damask chair. I wished he had remained in the kitchen with his body.

"Maybe he tripped on a box and fell on the sword?" one of the officers in the kitchen asked.

"And threw it into the box in a fit of rage before he keeled over?" another scoffed. "Right."

An Officer Adams joined me in the dining room, looking around in vain for a place to sit and finally just leaning against a buffet stacked high with plates and lamps. He got out a notepad and pencil, then asked me to recount what had happened. I explained about my cat and my previous visits to Mr. Peter's house, about how I'd heard Taco inside, and when I'd seen the blood, I'd thought maybe my neighbor had fallen and needed help.

"And the blood on your hands?" he asked.

I really wanted to wipe it off, but there wasn't anything nearby, and I didn't think it would be polite to wipe bloody handprints on the boxes. Hopefully they would let me wash them soon, because my emotional numbness was starting to wear off, and the sticky feel on my fingers hinted toward a looming panic attack.

"I tried to see if he was breathing or had a pulse." I looked at my hands and swallowed hard. "I wasn't sure and he was facedown, so I thought if I could turn him over, I could..."

What, do mouth-to-mouth? CPR? I needed to wash my hands. I had to get this off my hands.

"Did you have any problems with Mr. Peter? Any disagreements beyond him feeding your cat?"

Was I hearing him right? There was no way this police officer was insinuating that I had anything to do with my neighbor's death. Murder. It was a murder, although I didn't really want to think about that right now with blood on my hands and his body one room away. Clearly, he'd fallen on the sword by accident.

"No. He was going to fix up a vintage toaster for me. Just yesterday he'd given me an appraisal on a pitcher my husband and I had received as a wedding gift. And I wasn't angry about the cat. Well, I was a bit angry *at* the cat, but not at Mr. Peter. He was a lonely guy who clearly had his problems, but I never had any issues with him."

The officer scribbled some notes. "Anyone else you know have any disagreements with Mr. Peter?"

My heart sank. "Yes. Nobody liked the junk in his yard, of course. A few years ago, when the Millers were selling, they tried to get the city to condemn the property to force him out, and Will Lars next door has been frustrated because he's opening a B&B and all the junk deters people from wanting to stay at his inn." I thought for a second. "Oh, and Friday, Mr. Peter's nephew came by and argued with him. I think he's been trying to get his uncle to go into assisted living."

Scribble. Scribble. "Anyone else?"

"Yes. I mean, look at the place." *There is blood on my hands. There is blood on my hands.* "We all work hard to keep our houses and property nice, and it's difficult having this mess smack in the middle of our block. But being upset because someone has broken washing machines all over their front lawn isn't the same as wanting him or her dead. If you think that's the motive, then half the neighborhood and more would be suspects, including the electric company guy who, when Mr. Peter doesn't chase him off, has to run an obstacle course every time he comes to read the meter."

"You'd be surprised at what is often a motive for murder," the officer commented dryly. "Did you touch anything except for the body? The sword? We'll need to print you so we can exclude your fingerprints."

At least they were no longer considering me a suspect based on an alleged wandering-cat-feud. But at the mention of fingerprints, I'd looked down and was now on edge over the blood on my hands. It was sticky, but was drying into a cold, hard crust on my fingers. Would it stain? Would I be standing at the sink, scrubbing my hands raw like Lady Macbeth as I tried to wash it off?

What had the officer asked? Oh, yeah. "No. I mean, I may have balanced myself on some boxes coming in, and I did have to climb over that dresser to get to the kitchen, but after I touched Mr. Peter, I didn't touch anything else. Except my phone." Oh no. My phone probably had blood on it as well. It was a wonder I'd managed to get the touch screen to work.

"Not the sword?"

"Not the sword," I repeated, putting some emphasis in the statement. I might have touched something that I could no longer remember, but I was positive that I hadn't touched the sword. "Oh, but my cat was probably all over everything. He's got blood on his fur. That's how I knew something was wrong. That's why I came into the house. It's not like I make a habit of walking into my neighbors' houses uninvited, you know. I'm not a thief or anything. My cat had blood on his fur, and Mr. Peter didn't answer when I knocked. I was concerned."

And I was rambling. No wonder criminals got caught all the time. I wasn't even in an interrogation room and I was singing like a canary. Of course, criminals were probably calmer under pressure than I was. I'm sure the murderer wasn't staring at his hands, fighting off a panic attack and wondering if nail polish remover might help get the blood out. Or maybe he was, for all I knew.

"Kay?" Judge Beck appeared in the doorway, his brow creased in concern. "What's going on? I came home to

Madison in hysterics because Taco is covered in blood and half a dozen police cars are across the street from our home."

Our home. In spite of my being at the edge of a panic attack, my heart grew ten times its size at that. My parents were gone. Eli's parents were gone. Neither of us had siblings, and we'd never had children. Was I so starved for family that I was ready to cling onto Judge Beck and his children like a lifeline? I hoped that this, like the shadows, was a product of grief, because he would be leaving in two years, moving out and buying a place of his own, and unlike *real* family, they most likely wouldn't keep in touch beyond the occasional Christmas card or an invitation to a graduation party.

"Mr. Peter was murdered." I was proud at how steady my voice was. "Although I heard the police mention they thought he might have fallen on his sword."

I don't know why I added that ridiculous idea. Perhaps to soften the thought of a murder directly across the street from my home—from our home.

The judge's face froze in shock. "Fell on his sword? Like seppuku-style? Was he Japanese? I don't think I've ever even seen the man."

Officer Adams glared at Judge Beck, then must have recognized him because his expression quickly shifted to one of wary respect. "No, sir. It's clearly a murder, although we'll wait for the M.E. report to deliver the official announcement."

"Now Mrs. Carrera," he continued. "You say you've been here before. Did you notice if anything is missing?"

A theft? Who in the world would be foolish enough to steal from a hoarder? They'd need six months and a backhoe to find anything of value among the cases of toilet paper and broken appliances.

"Um, I'm not sure. Things seemed to have been moved

around a bit, but from what Mr. Peter told me, he got new china in and rotated what he liked to 'display' up front near the door. He did say he had some valuable Faience upstairs in a bedroom, but I've never actually seen it, and by Mr. Peter's standards, everything in the house was valuable."

The officer made another quick note, then flicked his fingers, extending a business card toward me like he was a sleight-of-hand magician. "Thank you. If you remember anything else, please call us."

I guessed that was my dismissal. I looked around, trying to find the best way out of the house that wouldn't either compromise the crime scene or send me to the hospital with a broken ankle.

"Should I go out the back door?" I pointed. Unlike my house, Mr. Peter didn't have the door in the kitchen leading to the rear of the house. His was at the back of a little room off from the former dining room that I was standing in.

The officer looked over at the door. "I guess. You'll need to move those boxes. And I'm not sure if it opens or not."

I wasn't, either. The wood might have swollen to the point that the door was wedged tight in the jamb, or painted shut. What happened to a door that didn't get used in a few years or decades?

In spite of the implication that I'd need to move the boxes myself, the officer began to clear a path to the door. We set up a sort of fire brigade, where he'd hand me the box, then I'd hand it to Judge Beck who would look around, trying to find a place to put it where one more box wouldn't send a tower toppling to the floor.

One box opened from the bottom in the officer's hands and he shoved his knee upward, catching the contents before they dropped and shattered on the floor.

"Here." I reached underneath to ease what looked to be a Tiffany-style lamp from the box. At least I thought it was

Tiffany-style. For all I knew, it could have been the real thing. It made me wonder how much in this house was actual expensive antiques and how much was just old reproductions.

Judge Beck frowned at the lamp as he took it from my hand. "I know this is a safe neighborhood, but is this a case where we should be worried about looters? Has anyone called this man's next of kin? Does he have any sort of security system?"

The officer tested the structural integrity of the next box, then opened the top and began to pull out a set of glass plates with a diamond pattern around the edges. "We haven't figured out who the next of kin is yet, sir. And as far as we can tell, there's no security system, just a simple lock on the doorknob."

"Nosy neighbors are the best security," I told him. "And we've got the nosiest here."

"I'm hoping someone was extra nosy and saw who came and went from Mr. Peter's house between the hours of four and nine," he commented, handing me the plates.

Four and nine? That didn't sound right. "It was probably later than that. The front door wasn't ajar when I got here. Someone let my cat into this house, and he didn't escape mine earlier than six o'clock. Probably closer to seven."

His eyebrows shot up and he paused to pull the notebook out and jot my comment down. "Are you positive, Mrs. Carrera?"

"Yes. Taco was inside when I went to get the cake from the kitchen at six. I think one of the girls might have accidently let him out. We noticed he was gone at seven-thirty. When the girls left at a little before nine and he hadn't come back, I suspected he'd come over here. Mr. Peter used to feed him chicken sandwiches." My voice hitched a little on the last few words. He'd really liked my cat. It was sad that he'd not be able to spoil Taco with his leftovers any more. As if sensing my distress, the shadow moved from the damask chair back into the kitchen. Good. I hoped he stayed there.

I thought for a moment. The time window meant either Mr. Peter had been alive to let Taco in at six to around seven tonight, or that the murderer had let the cat in as he was leaving. I closed my eyes for a second, imagining the different scenarios. If Mr. Peter had let Taco in, the cat could have run and hid during the actual murder, not coming out until after the killer had left. Or if the murderer was here earlier, Taco could have darted between his legs as he left. He wouldn't want to waste time or risk getting caught to track down a cat in a house packed full of boxes and junk, so he just closed the door and left Taco on the inside.

"Here."

I popped my eyes open to see the officer handing me another box. The door was now in view. Setting the last box aside, Judge Beck squeezed past me and assisted the officer in getting the stuck door to open. He flicked a switch by the window, but no light came on in the backyard.

"I've got it." Judge Beck pulled his phone out and tapped the screen. The flashlight app illuminated only about five feet in front of us. Handy, but we'd still need to be careful.

The officer left the door open to allow the inside light to spill out into a back yard that looked like a set from a post-apocalyptic movie. In addition to the lawnmowers, stoves, and refrigerators, there were rusted motorcycles, two dilapidated cars up on cinder blocks, and two sheds, one of which had collapsed from rot. Around the yard was a stockade-style fence that was propped up in some sections with two-by-four braces, and just allowed to sag in others. The whole mess was overgrown with tall grass, vines, and something I was pretty sure was poison ivy.

I was feeling pretty sorry for Will Lars right now, as well

as the Tennisons who lived on the other side of Mr. Peter. The fence would block the mess, but from the upstairs windows, both neighbors would have a clear view of this disaster.

"It's going to take his heirs a year to haul all this stuff out," Judge Beck muttered as he cautiously made his way down the warped wooden stairs.

"Probably. Get used to the idea of a huge dumpster outside on the street for a while." I declined his offered hand, because I wasn't unsteady on my feet. If these stairs were going to collapse, there was no need to drag him down with me.

Judge Beck looked around the yard. I caught a quick glimpse of his expression in the cell phone light and was surprised to see that instead of looking disgusted, he appeared sad.

"Poor guy. There are people at county Adult Services that would have helped him if he'd just reached out."

"He didn't think he needed help. He was happy with all his stuff, although I think he was a bit lonely. And he missed being useful."

We fell silent, picking our way through the maze of junk and weeds, trying to avoid the poison ivy. When we reached the less-crowded front part of the lawn, I felt a sense of relief as if I'd successfully navigated a minefield.

"So that's two in three months, Kay," Judge Beck commented. "Are you now the murder-victim whisperer?"

"I see dead people," I deadpanned. The irony was I was beginning to believe that I did see dead people. Hopefully this didn't give Judge Beck any hesitation in my being around his children, or about my house being a safe place for them. "In my defense, the murderers are gone when I find their victims. It's not like I'm walking in on them in the act or something."

He shot me a quick backward look. "Didn't the mayor try to kill you?"

I'd forgotten about that. Which wasn't normally a thing that would slip someone's mind. "Just that once. Although I think that should be bragging rights, don't you agree? How many people can say that their town mayor tried to murder them?"

It had been terrifying, which was why I had to make light of it. Otherwise, I'd wind up having a panic attack and that did no one any good.

"Let's stick to the 'finding victim' part this time," he commented.

"I'm hoping the 'finding victim' thing ends with this one. Twice in one lifetime is plenty." And having the mayor point a loaded gun at me once in my lifetime was plenty as well. Although our mayor was now in jail, and I doubted that he had anything to do with poor Mr. Peter's demise.

But who did? The nephew? I knew he was frustrated with all the complaints about his uncle, but I couldn't imagine he'd go from yelling at the elderly man on his front porch to murdering in twenty-four hours. And Will Lars…had he been told by the city inspectors that there was nothing they could do about the condition of the property? It wasn't like Mr. Peter was throwing the old washing machines on *their* lawn. Had Will's irritation with the situation driven him to murder? I just couldn't see him running a sword through Mr. Peter.

But as the officer had said, who knew what people could do in the heat of anger?

Madison and Henry were waiting on my front porch. The girl had Taco in her arms, still damp from a bath that he'd probably hated with every fiber of his being. I saw as I climbed the steps that her eyes were puffy from crying, and that Henry looked as if he'd been the one who'd found the dead body.

I looked down at the dried blood on my hands and stuffed them behind my back. "Why don't we all sit in the living room for a bit. I'll make some cocoa and break out the leftover cake."

The mention of cake brightened Henry up considerably and we all filed in the door. I made my way to the kitchen and was grateful that, unlike Lady Macbeth, the blood did wash off fairly easily. Armed with mugs of instant cocoa and a plate with slices of pound cake, I went into the living room. Madison was still clutching Taco, who looked to be dozing off in her lap. Henry jumped up when I arrived, helping me put the cake and mugs down before taking one for himself.

I grabbed a mug of my own and sat down. "I don't know what you've pieced together, but I'll tell you what I know."

It was good for the kids to have all the details, all the facts. I'd discovered that sometimes what an imaginative mind can make up was far more frightening than what truly happened.

"Is it Mr. Peter?" Henry whispered, eyes huge. "Is he…dead?"

I nodded. "Taco liked to go over there because Mr. Peter would feed him bits of his chicken sandwiches. He got out during our party, and when he didn't come back, I was pretty sure he was across the street getting his chicken fix."

Madison let out a laugh, then clapped a hand over her mouth. Judge Beck frowned, but I smiled at her reassuringly.

"No one answered when I knocked on the door, but I could hear Taco meowing inside the house. After a while, I got worried that something might have happened to Mr. Peter, that maybe he'd fallen and couldn't get to the door, so I went in. I found him in his kitchen. He had already passed away by the time I got there."

"But Taco was covered in blood," Madison said softly.

I eyed Judge Beck. As much as I wanted to tell the kids everything, they were his children, not mine. He hesitated a second, then nodded for me to go on.

"Sadly, Mr. Peter did not die of natural causes. He was attacked…stabbed."

Both Madison and Henry sucked in a shocked breath.

"Although what happened to Mr. Peter is technically a murder, I don't believe there is any cause for either of you to be frightened," Judge Beck added. "I've seen many murder cases come across my bench, and I'm certain this one had a personal side to it."

"So, no one is going around robbing houses and killing people?" Henry asked. "Although if I were going to rob someone, it wouldn't be Mr. Peter. I really don't think that the burglar would be able to find anything of value to steal unless he planned to be there for a few weeks or more."

"Burglars tend to rob houses when no one is home," Judge Beck told him. "I'm fairly certain this isn't the beginning of a spree of breaking and entering."

Madison lifted a sleepy Taco and buried her face in his fur. "Poor Taco. Were you trying to help Mr. Peter? Is that how you got blood all over you?"

It was more likely that my cat had gotten blood on him while trying to steal the chicken sandwich out of a dead man's hand, but I didn't want to be the one to shatter the girl's fantasies. "I'm sure Taco is devastated. And no, you cannot start giving him chicken sandwiches to console him in his grief. He's on a diet."

Madison whispered something to the cat that I was pretty sure included a promise to sneak him all sorts of goodies. She was still clutching him when Judge Beck herded them all up the stairs. As much as I'd miss the cat in my bedroom tonight…if he'd bring Madison some comfort, then he could stay with her.

As for me, there was no way I could sleep right now. I wasn't sure I'd sleep at all tonight. Eyeing the decanter of whisky on the bookshelf, I wondered if it would help chase the images of Mr. Peter out of my head. As I weighed the pros and cons, I saw a shadow move in the corner of my eye, approaching and hovering by the sofa. This shadow was so very familiar, not like the one I'd seen across the street tonight. This shadow was mine.

"Eli?" I whispered. If he'd been alive, we would have talked about what happened. Well, I would have talked and Eli would have interjected odd random observations and what sometimes seemed like existential advice. But he would have known I was upset, and comforted me with his presence.

And before the accident, that Eli and I would have talked— both of us. He would have listened intently, asked questions, helped me organize the thoughts that were racing around my brain from the shock of finding a neighbor dead with a bloody sword nearby. He would have soothed me with his logic, comforted me with his love. Then he would have fixed me a glass of whisky and had one himself—because pre-accident Eli never turned down a whisky—and held me in his arms.

Both Elis would have comforted me in their own way.

I got up and reached for the whisky. "Do you want one, too?" I asked the shadow.

"Yes, please."

I about jumped out of my skin until I realized that the words had come from Judge Beck and not my ghostly apparition.

Taking a deep breath to calm my jangled nerves, I grabbed two of the cut-glass tumblers and the decanter, carrying it all over to the sofa. There I sat pouring two fingers in each glass and handing one to the judge. I'd expected him to take the wingback chair he'd occupied previously, but instead he sat next to me on the sofa.

"Are the kids okay?" I asked.

"The kids are fine. Are *you* okay, Kay? I came in with the M.E. and saw everything in the kitchen. I can't believe you walked in on that."

I sipped the whisky, relishing the honeyed burn as it slid down my throat, feeling the slight numb calmness it elicited when it hit my nervous system. It had been shocking to see Mr. Peter like that. But then again, it had been shocking to see Caryn Swanson's body in that watery ditch a few months ago.

But Mr. Peter…I knew him. He was a neighbor. This was so close to home, close to my safe space. As horrible as it had been to discover that a young woman had been murdered, this was somehow worse.

"I'll be all right. Tomorrow is Sunday, so after yoga with Daisy, I'll read or knit and try to put it out of my mind."

Or maybe I should go to church? I wasn't one to attend service weekly, preferring to keep my devotions to myself, but this might be one of those occasions where praising Our Lord in the presence of others might bring comfort. And I did want to speak with Reverend Lincoln about grief and ghosts, and my nightly visitor, the shadow who had retreated in Judge Beck's presence to stand over by the bookshelf. If I squinted, I could almost imagine he was Eli, elbow on one shelf as he shifted his weight to the side and watched me.

"Kay?"

"What?" Sheesh. Judge Beck was going to think I'd totally lost my mind.

"I'm planning to take the kids out for ice cream tomorrow afternoon. Would you join us?"

Again, I got that surge of hope, of happiness that they were including me, that they'd somehow be my family. I shouldn't be doing this. I shouldn't let myself get too attached to them.

But it was too late. I was already attached. And an afternoon eating soft serve with jimmies wasn't going to change that.

"Thank you. That sounds wonderful; I'd love to go."

Then we sat on the sofa next to each other, sipping whisky in silence. And when our glasses were empty, we wished each other a good night and climbed the stairs. And as I got ready for bed I realized two things. The shadow had left sometime while I'd been lost in thought on the couch, and I was really looking forward to ice cream tomorrow.

CHAPTER 9

" $\mathcal{H}$ e was dead? As in bleeding out on the floor? Was he still warm? Had rigor set in?"

Daisy had maintained a respectful silence while we'd completed our morning yoga routine, but she wasn't shy about destroying the brief peace I'd obtained with her questions right after we'd finished the last vinyasa.

"You really should stop with the police shows, Daisy. As far as I could tell, he was done bleeding when I'd found him. I don't remember if he was warm or not. And I've got no idea if rigor had set in. Sorry, but my amateur crime-scene investigation plans flew right out the window when I walked into the kitchen and found my neighbor dead, a bloody sword rammed through a cardboard box next to him."

There. That should be enough shocking details to satisfy even Daisy.

"A sword? Who kills someone with a sword anymore? I mean, I can see where you wouldn't want to draw attention to a murder-in-process by firing a gun in a quiet neighborhood, but why didn't the killer hit him on the head with a frying pan, or bludgeon him with a meat cleaver?"

Ugh. Days like this, I really wondered about the mental stability of my best friend. I grabbed two mugs and headed for the coffee pot, wishing that I knew how to change the conversation. But that was an impossibility when Daisy was digging for information.

"Well, I'm going to say that in a hoarder's house, it might take quite a while to find a frying pan or a meat cleaver. The sword was right there, on top of a stack of boxes by the doorway. It was handy."

Wait. It was by the doorway. And it had been there the second time I'd come back. So, the killer had grabbed it by the door, but had stabbed Mr. Peter in the kitchen. Had he chased him into the kitchen? Or had he picked up the sword when he'd entered the house and snuck back to the kitchen, intent on murder? It made a difference, because this couldn't be self-defense gone wrong, where the two struggled, and the killer just reached out and grabbed the first thing handy. No. If the sword had been in a completely different room, then there was intent and there was some planning involved, at least from the time of entry to the actual stabbing.

"Wow. A murder, right on our street. I mean, there are plenty of times I thought that Harry Peter was going to wind up strangled, or possibly crushed by a falling stack of washing machines, but I never imagined he'd be stabbed to death. And with a sword."

Daisy's words gave me pause. Sometimes it was good to be best friends with an incorrigible gossip.

"All right then, let's list the likely suspects. I'll start —Will Lars."

Daisy laughed, stirring cream into her coffee. "With a sword? Don't get me wrong, Will has a temper and he's one of those guys who, once he's got his mind set on something, isn't about to be dissuaded. He's not the most flexible guy in the world. I don't think he's ever heard the word compromise in his entire life. It's one of the reasons he got fired from that last job. He's determined to make a go of it with this bed and breakfast, and he's absolutely obsessed with every little detail. Having a neighbor with a junkyard isn't in his action plan for success, if you know what I mean."

"But when they bought the place, Mr. Peter had already been living there. Did the real estate agent show them the place in the middle of the night? Did she blindfold them until they got inside? How could Will not have known that he was buying a house next to a large appliance hoarder?"

"That was when the Millers were selling and the city had slapped Harry Peter with a code violation. Will thought between that and the guy's age that he'd either move or die within the year. And their place was priced accordingly. Kat makes good money, but neither of them had a big down payment. That house was a bit of a stretch for them as it was." She shrugged. "They took a gamble that Harry Peter would be gone and his yard and home fixed up before they either got ready to sell or Will went too crazy staring at it each day. Him losing his job and starting the inn just pushed the timetable forward."

And upped the stress. "You sure you want to cross him off of our suspect list? Sounds like he had motive, and if he's the hot-tempered type..."

Daisy rolled her eyes. "Not *that* kind of hot-tempered, though. I could see him getting mad and throwing something that accidently knocked old man Peter's brains out, but not running him through with a sword. Although if Harry made him really, really mad, then who knows." She sipped her coffee. "I think Kat's going to leave if Will doesn't settle the heck down. It's not just the money thing. She loves him, but he's driving her crazy obsessing over the inn. Having their house as a business? Having him home all day, hounding her about keeping the house perfect, wanting her to bake muffins for the guests and crochet doilies as gifts…I give her two months and she'll be stuffing suitcases in the car and heading to her sister's."

So Will definitely had a motive. He'd never admit that it was him driving Kat away. No, he'd blame the money. And the solution to the money issue was to make the inn profitable. And the solution to that was getting their hoarder neighbor to clean up at least the front and backyards.

"Okay, I'm leaving Will on the list. How about the nephew?"

"Bert Peter? I guess. I think he loved his uncle at one time, but five years ago the old guy threw a toaster at him. Poor guy had to get stitches on Christmas Eve. Bert, I mean, not Harry."

"Christmas Eve?"

"Yeah. From what I could hear, and trust me, the whole neighborhood could hear. I'm surprised you weren't privy to this one. Anyway, Bert had come to take his uncle out to midnight Mass, which is a nice thing to do. But Old Man Peter decided that Bert was trying to lure him out of the house so he could sneak in and steal some fancy-pants stuff he had in the back room or the basement or something."

Yikes. "It seems like a stretch to stab an uncle for throwing a toaster at you five years ago, though."

Daisy nodded. "Yeah, but Bert's all he's got, I mean had. Harry dies and Bert gets everything, including the fancy-pants stuff in the basement. I don't know how much that stuff is worth, but the house is paid off, and judging from the UPS deliveries every day, I'm thinking the old guy had one heck of a savings account."

I thought for a second. "Okay, then why stab him with a sword? Why not just dump a bunch of his blood pressure meds in his coffee, or replace them with NoDoz or something? And the sword through the box seems kind of emotional, not a cold-blooded murder for inheritance."

"Maybe the UPS guy killed him because he's sick of hauling heavy boxes of junk through a maze of old washing machines." Daisy wiggled her eyebrows as if she'd just solved the crime.

"Maybe Harry Peter was single-handedly keeping the UPS guy in business," I countered.

"Maybe it was the meter-reading guy."

"Maybe it was Miss Scarlet in the library with a candlestick."

"Or Colonel Mustard. I always thought he had a shifty-eyed look about him."

I slugged down the rest of my coffee. "I hate to kick you out, but I need to get going if I'm going to make the ten o'clock service. Wanna come to church with me?"

Daisy shuddered. "Are you kidding? Naked in the middle of a forest, that's how I worship. Say a prayer for my soul, okay?"

"I always do. And don't forget your film debut tomorrow. J.T. is expecting you at the office bright and early to play your part."

I'd been checking up on my boss's YouTube video over the weekend, watching it over and over to boost the views. Surprisingly, it had a few hundred followers, although most of them were probably local police and friends he'd cornered into being extras. I wasn't sure why Daisy had accepted the invitation. She was normally pretty good at saying 'no' in a voice that brooked no argument. Instead she'd seemed flattered, as if J.T. hadn't asked half the town to play a part in his dramatic reenactments. Maybe my friend harbored secret dreams of making it big in Hollywood.

Daisy finished her coffee and I escorted her to the door, just so I could hold Taco while she left. I no longer had to worry about Mr. Peter feeding him chicken sandwiches, but I was oddly reluctant to let the cat out of my house.

He'd been in my neighbor's home at the scene of a murder. I just wanted him safe in my house, safe in my arms. As Madison had done last night, I cuddled him up to my face, feeling him purr as I watched Daisy walk down the sidewalk.

I was safe in my house, relaxed after yoga, energized from the coffee, feeling loved after spending the early morning hours with Daisy, and comforted by Taco's soft fur and the knowledge that upstairs slept Judge Beck, Madison, and Henry. My family, whether they knew it or not.

.

CHAPTER 10

$\mathscr{I}$'d been so tempted to just stay home and read or knit while sitting in the garden, but by the time the church bells rang at noon, and we'd all filtered out of the sanctuary, I was glad I'd showered, put on a dress, and hauled myself to the ten o'clock service.

Reverend Lincoln shook my hand and I waited out in the foyer for him to finish speaking to each of the parishioners as they left the service. When it was clear things had quieted down, I approached him with an apologetic smile.

"Do you have a moment, Reverend? I was hoping I could speak to you."

He turned to his assistant minister and asked him to finish up, then ushered me down the hall into his office. I sat, and instead of sitting on the other side of the desk, he eased himself down into the chair beside me.

"How are you doing, Kay?" He took one of my hands and gave it a quick squeeze.

I knew exactly what he meant. This had been Eli's and my church, although we hadn't attended more than three or four times a year. When my husband had died, Reverend Lincoln had delivered a beautiful service and eulogy. Just thinking about it brought tears to my eyes. It was probably one of the reasons I hadn't been to church since the funeral. Being here, seeing the minister, just brought that day all back to my mind. Fresh. As if Eli had taken his last breath in my arms all over again.

"There are days where I think I'm fine, where I feel the sunshine on my face and look at my cat and am glad to be alive. And there are days…well, there are days when I'm not doing so well. I have roommates now. They help."

He smiled. "Judge Beck and his two children. I was so glad to hear that you were able to work things out. Being able to keep your home, having close friends to ease you through this time of transition, it's all important."

I nodded, not sure how to approach the topic I wanted to discuss, so instead I skirted around it. "I'm worried that I've started thinking of Judge Beck and his kids as family. My parents have passed away and so have Eli's. We were only children and had no children of our own. I'm scared that with his loss, I'm latching onto a substitute family, and that it's inappropriate. I'm their landlord, their roommate. I know that Judge Beck considers me as a sort of friend, and Madison and Henry think of me as an honorary aunt or grandma or something, but when his divorce is final, he'll leave. And in two years, Madison will graduate high school and leave. They'll all leave and it's going to break my heart because in the next two years I'm going to become even more attached to them. I can't help it."

"That happens even with family, Kay. I can't tell you how many of my flock I've consoled when their children have gone off to college, or have gotten married and moved away. By the time they're in their seventies, they're lucky if they get a call on major holidays and a visit once per week."

"That isn't making me feel any better," I told him.

He laughed. "What I mean is that you can't hold back from connecting with people, from forming meaningful relationships and attachments out of fear that one day they might drift away. If this happens even with children and parents, then there's a risk it will happen with friendships and honorary relative relationships."

I tried to take his words to heart. "But who will I have then?"

"Did you have Judge Beck and his children three months ago? No. You'll continue to develop new attachments to different people as times goes on, Kay. If you're lucky, there will be people who are there for you throughout the majority of your life, but you need to trust that God will send you who you need, that if one person leaves your life, he'll give you someone to fill that emotional gap. Trust in your faith, trust in the Lord to not leave you lonely."

I thought of Daisy who had stood by me for so long. Then I thought of Mr. Peter across the street, who'd obviously been lonely and feeling a loss of self-worth. Where had God been for him? But he'd thrown a toaster at his nephew. Maybe he hadn't been willing to accept those that God sent him.

And there was me. And Taco. I remembered how happy Mr. Peter had been holding my cat, calling him Taco-schmacko and spoiling him with bits of chicken sandwiches. I remembered his excitement when I brought the pitcher by. How his eyes had lit up at the thought of fixing up an antique toaster and mixer for me. Maybe right there at the end, Mr. Peter had felt that sense of friendship, of comradery that he'd denied himself for years—maybe even decades.

"I'll try," I told Reverend Lincoln. "I'll try, but I'm scared."

"Of course you're scared. I'd be surprised if you weren't. Ten years ago, your life was turned upside down when Eli had that accident. Honestly, Kay, I don't think you've ever really recovered from that blow... You just threw yourself into Eli's care and never truly grieved or came to terms with how that accident changed *your* life as well as his. Then after all those years of burying your feelings and emotions, Eli passes away and suddenly you're faced with it all. It's like grieving in double-time. I know you're scared, but from my vantage point, you're handling it remarkably well. You're finally able to grieve, and you're using your support network and making new friends and close relationships to help you weather the storm. I'm here for you, Kay. I know you're not someone who likes to attend service every Sunday, but I'm here for you during the week as well."

This *was* making me feel better—it was making me feel strong enough to broach the topic that had brought me to church today.

"I see ghosts. Is that a problem? Because I think the main ghost I'm seeing is Eli, but I see other ghosts. I've discovered two murder victims in the last three months and each time I've seen ghosts. My ophthalmologist at first thought it was floaters from my cataract surgery, but this last appointment he recommended I talk to you or to a grief therapist."

My minster stared at me, obviously struggling to process what I'd just said. "Floaters. So, you're seeing blurry round shadows as an optical condition?"

"No. These are shadows. They're humanoid in shape and always in the corner of my vision. I can't quite focus on them but I can see them and in the last few months, they've become more distinct. There's one that is around mostly in the evenings, especially in my house although he's sometimes with me while I'm out shopping or at work. That's the one I think might be Eli's ghost. But the other two...they appeared when I discovered the murder victims."

"Kay, I truly think that grief and loneliness can bring a person to imagine their lost loved one as being present.

That's normal and, in time, these imaginings will lessen. As for the other two...well, I think that shock can sometimes bring the mind to see things that aren't there."

He didn't believe me. Well, he believed me, but thought it was part of processing my grief and shock. If he'd experienced what I had on a daily basis, then maybe he'd have something different in mind than "it's normal".

"But with the one murder victim, I saw the ghost *before* I discovered the body. Before I even had the idea that there could be a body."

He thought for a moment. "Describe when you saw the first ghost."

I thought back to when I'd found Caryn Swanson's body. I'd been returning to my car in the parking lot of MegaMart. "I always park way in the back section, so I can get a little exercise in going to and from the store. There was this sudden patch of cold. The sky seemed to dim. Then I saw the ghost. After the ghost vanished, I saw a shoe by the edge of the parking area where a hill led down to a draining ditch and the highway. That's where the body was."

He nodded. "What if you saw the shoe, but hadn't quite registered it yet? Your unconscious mind saw a woman's shoe and thought the worst because you yourself had just suffered a loss and it was fresh in your mind?"

"I guess so." Maybe. I was sure I hadn't seen the shoe before the ghost, but maybe he was right.

"And the second one?"

"Taco had made a habit of visiting the guy across the street. He's elderly and a hoarder and he would feed him. Taco snuck out one night and I went to get him, but no one answered the door and I heard my cat inside, so I let myself in. I saw the ghost right after I went into the kitchen and discovered his body."

The minister smiled and patted my hand. "Weren't you

worried? He was elderly. He hadn't answered the door when you knocked. I doubt you would have just walked into his house if you hadn't been worried that something had happened to him. Again, your concern thought of the worst. And since you'd lost Eli and a few months earlier had discovered a murder victim, you immediately imagined the worst. And that imagination manifested as what you think of as a ghost. Kay, this is completely normal. You have experienced three deaths in four months. It's going to be the first thing that comes to your mind for some time. It's going to be your worst-case-scenario for a while."

Maybe he was right. "So you don't believe in ghosts? Or you just don't think that what I'm experiencing are ghosts but something else entirely?"

He thought for a moment. "Our souls leave this world when we die. Ghosts are manifestations of our grief or fear or guilt. They're the product of strong emotion, but they have nothing to do with the person who has died. The ghost at your house isn't Eli's spirit. It's just your way of processing his loss."

I sighed, not sure whether his words were a relief or whether I'd be happier to know what I was experiencing was a spirit. I didn't want to tie Eli to this world, but I did miss him, and I did feel that there was a lot of unfinished business in our relationship. But perhaps that was why my mind was conjuring a shadow.

"So what should I do? How do you recommend I deal with these…ghosts, for want of a better term?"

"I think whenever you see one, especially the one that you identify as Eli, you need to examine your emotions at the time, as well as the situation. Were you doing something that reminded you of your husband, that you used to do together? Were you feeling vulnerable or lonely, or wishing for his company, advice, or comfort? Once you've identified that, just let yourself feel. Miss him. Feel the ache of his loss in your life. Remember that there are others who can give you company, advice, and comfort in his stead. They'll never replace him, but you don't need to be empty without him."

Let myself grieve. It was hard. I felt like I'd be grieving forever, like I'd never recover from Eli's death. And Reverend Lincoln was right. I'd not been able to really deal with the turmoil of the accident, so I was grieving double.

It was so painful that sometimes I worried that if I let myself go, if I allowed myself to truly face what I'd lost, that I'd never recover. I could only take grief in little bits at a time. Maybe that meant it would take me longer to heal than others, maybe that's was why I saw these 'ghosts', but it was better than falling down into a well so deep that I'd never be able to climb up again.

I stood and Reverend Lincoln did the same, giving me a quick hug. "Be gentle with yourself, Kay. And remember, family is anyone who loves you. And you, my dear, are very, very loved."

CHAPTER 11

I eyed Henry's ice cream, most of which was surrounding his mouth like a chocolate beard and mustache. He'd insisted on the extra-large cone, and was struggling to keep pace with the melting—struggling and failing.

"Dork. I told you to get it in a cup," Madison told him. She'd chosen a banana split and was trying to chop up the banana so that she could get a tiny sliver in each bite.

"Miss Kay is going to make you hose off outside before you go in the house," Judge Beck teased his son. He'd been reluctant to order anything for himself, but the kids badgered him until he got a butterscotch sundae with nuts and whipped cream.

Myself, I was more of a hot fudge woman. As in extra hot fudge. I think I would have been happy if they had just filled the cup with hot fudge and foregone the ice cream, but I needed to at least make an attempt to appear civilized. No cherry. No whipped cream. No nuts. Just a gallon of hot fudge on my creamy-smooth soft serve vanilla ice cream.

"Forget the hose, I'll just toss you in the hot tub," I told Henry.

"Ewww." Madison wrinkled her nose. "That's disgusting. He'll make the water dirty with all that ice cream."

There were enough chemicals in there to take care of any health-related concerns, but I noticed that Henry seemed to not be hearing either his father's teasing, or mine and Madison's comments. I turned and followed his gaze across the parking lot, wondering what had captured his attention. We were eating at the open-air metal benches outside of the Tastee Cone which was opposite a shopping center. Henry was either staring at the grocery store, the liquor store, any number of spiffy cars that were assembled in an impromptu car show at the edge of the lot, or the people milling about the impromptu car show.

"Is everything all right?" I asked him softly.

He jerked his head, giving me a sheepish smile. "Yeah. I just think...that guy over there with the Mustang is someone I know. I think that's Dillon Buckle."

I looked again. The guy standing next to the Mustang was a man in his mid-twenties with a hairstyle that brought back memories of Flock of Seagulls. He was tall and thin, wearing a pair of white skinny jeans and a pastel striped loose-fit tank top. It was the kind of tank top where the sleeve holes were big enough to drive a full-size pickup truck through them, and in my opinion, the guy didn't have the muscular body type to pull it off. But who was I to judge other people's fashion choices?

"Nice car," I commented. It was. That Mustang looked brand new and seemed to be outfitted with all the bells and whistles. I felt a moment of envy. Not that I wanted a Mustang, but my twelve-year-old sedan probably didn't have more than a year or two left on it. I held my breath every time I went out to start it, praying that it wouldn't need more than an oil change, brakes, or new tires in the near future.

Henry squinted at the car. "Yeah, that's Dillon Buckle. He's Sean's sister's boyfriend, but I don't remember him having a car like that last time I saw him."

I looked the guy over once more. Sean was in track with Henry and was usually over once or twice per week. They'd play video games up in Henry's room, or go out and ride bikes all over the neighborhood. But Sean was thirteen, and I squirmed to think that a sister of his would be of an age to be dating a man in his mid-twenties. "How old is Sean's sister?"

"Twenty-three." Henry grinned at my surprised look. "Jessie is his half-sister. Sean's mom was married before."

I eyed Dillon Buckle again, wondering if he just had a really good job, or if he was one of those young people that blew every dime on a sweet car and ate Ramen every night.

We walked back to the car, and Henry and I lagged behind while he tried to wipe the worst of the ice cream from his face. The napkins weren't doing much good, but I'd found an ancient wet-wipe in my purse from some crab feast in another life and had given it to the boy.

"Miss Kay?" Henry asked, scrubbing his chin. "I think I might be the reason Taco was going over to Mr. Peter's house all the time."

"What, you got him hooked on chicken sandwiches and when you cut him off, he needed to find a new supplier?"

Henry looked at the wet-wipe, then rubbed his mouth again. "No, he started following me over there and hanging out with us. And Mr. Peter would give him snacks, so I think he got used to it."

I stopped in the parking lot. "You were going over to Mr. Peter's house?"

He squirmed, balling up the napkins and wet-wipe in his fist. "Right after we moved in, I was riding my bike and saw something cool in his yard, so I went to check it out. And then I saw something cool in his backyard. He saw me back there and I thought he'd be mad, 'cause old people don't like you trespassing, but he was really nice. He showed me some other stuff and offered me cookies and juice."

And now I was freaking out, imagining the most horrible things ever. Reverend Lincoln was wrong. Death wasn't my worst-case-scenario; the terrifying suspicions running through my mind right now were. "Does your dad know? Did he…what did he show you?"

"He showed me some cool old alarm clocks. Sheesh, Miss Kay, I'm not five. I can tell when people are being creepy and I know about bad-touch and all that. He was just a lonely old man. And he was nice. And no, I didn't tell my dad because I was sure he'd react the same way. I thought since you knew him, since you'd gone over there a few times, that you'd understand."

Henry's voice was getting louder, his face red.

"Okay, okay. I'm sorry. It's just that you're thirteen, and I didn't know you were going over there. And I didn't expect that a kid your age would be interested in old appliances and china."

The boy thrust his chin up. I noticed that there was still some ice cream smeared along the edge. "What am I *supposed* to like? I like running in track. I like gardening. I like riding my bike and video games and swimming. And I like old stuff. It's cool to look at something and think that someone's grandmother, or maybe Ben Franklin, or somebody else used it. It's cool to look at old stuff and wonder why people bought it, what they used it for, why they eventually got rid of it."

I'd stereotyped this poor kid. And if I'd realized he liked to garden, I would have put him to work three months ago.

"I'm so sorry, Henry. I don't have kids of my own, and I

was an only child growing up. It was a long time since I was your age, and I obviously have a lot of wrong ideas about what thirteen-year-old boys should be interested in."

He looked down at his hands. "It's okay. I don't think Dad understands either. He doesn't like gardening, or video games, or old stuff."

I put my arm around the boy's shoulder. "No, he likes law books. Yuck. I mean, who in their right mind would voluntarily read that stuff?"

He laughed. "I know, right?"

"You need to tell him, though. And if you want to hang out with any of our neighbors in the future, please let him know." Then something struck me. "It must be really hard for you that Mr. Peter died."

He nodded, still looking at the crumpled napkins. "He was a nice guy. I'm gonna miss him."

"I know. Me, too." We headed to the car, and I thought there was one more thing that God had sent Harry Peter in the sunset of his life—a young friend who shared his interests.

CHAPTER 12

"*H*ow many more gray hairs do I have since this morning?" Judge Beck asked.

I motioned for him to bend down and took a look. It was hard to tell what were sun-streaks in his blond hair and what was gray. Lucky duck. "Five," I finally announced. "That's pretty good. Madison's given you more."

He grimaced. "Madison is also fifteen. She wants me to allow Austin Meadows to take her to the movies next week. I'm trying to find a reason to say no."

"You can always insist on going with them and sitting two rows back." I tried and failed to hold back a smile.

"Don't laugh, I might do that. I'm just warning you in case I come home with snow-white hair."

"Or completely bald," I suggested. Judge Beck looked genuinely terrified at the prospect, and I did end up laughing.

"It's Henry who's causing me the gray hairs today. He said he told you about going over and 'hanging out' with Mr. Peter?" Judge Beck made little air quotes, as if 'hanging out' were some newfangled expression that he needed to emphasize.

"I know. I wigged out at first too, although there was never any rumor of Mr. Peter being anything but a nice old guy. Well, except for that time he threw a toaster at his nephew's head."

"He did *what?*" Judge Beck waved the question away. "Anyway, Henry swears nothing happened beyond the old man showing him a whole bunch of pottery and china and old appliances."

"That's pretty much what he did when I went over, except I wasn't interested enough to stay more than five minutes."

The judge sighed, running a hand through his not-so-gray hair. "Evidently Henry was interested enough to stay for a few hours—hours I thought he was out riding his bike. After the first visit, he said he brought Sean over with him, I guess as a sort of chaperone."

That was actually pretty smart. "Does Sean like antiques as well?" I hated to make assumptions, since I'd clearly been very wrong about Henry's interests and hobbies.

"No. But Sean is a good friend and evidently Mr. Peter gets the grocery store to deliver a selection of awesome cookies. Sean would raise his blood sugar levels through the roof while Mr. Peter and Henry discussed numerous old china brands that I've never heard of before." He shook his head. "I didn't know. I mean, what thirteen-year-old boy likes pottery and china?"

"A very well-adjusted boy," I replied.

"I get the old alarm clock thing. I liked to take electronic stuff apart myself when I was that age, too." Judge Beck shot me a knowing look. "And my incredible lack of skill in putting things back together resulted in my parents suggesting a career in law."

I laughed. "If it makes you feel any better, I don't think

Henry is interested in becoming a hoarder. I get the idea that he likes the history aspect of it all, likes the stories behind the pieces. He could end up a history professor, or maybe an author. Or maybe running a nursery."

Judge Beck did a double take. "He likes babies?"

"Not that kind of nursery. I meant plants. He said he really likes to garden."

He nodded. "When he was little, Heather would bring him outside with her when she was planting flowers around the house. Henry would pull weeds, and each year she'd give him a special flower to plant. It would be Henry's flower, and we made darned sure that no matter what, that flower got watered regularly."

"See? You both did good. Henry's learning what he likes and what he doesn't."

"But a gardener? Or an antiques dealer." The judge thought for a moment. "Although I like the idea of a professor. Tenure at a prestigious university. Papers published in a leading journal."

"Whoa, Dad. He might be teaching high school, or be an auctioneer. Don't pigeonhole the poor boy."

"You're right. Guess I'll need to pin my lawyer hopes on Madison."

I doubted that, given the conversation we'd had a few days ago, but didn't want to shatter yet another of Judge Beck's hopes and dreams. "Well, she did tell me that doctor is no longer on her short list after this AP chemistry class. Although I have to confess that she's asked me to show her how to bake."

Judge Beck looked so forlorn at my words that I took pity on him. "I'm sure lawyer is still in the running."

"Well, if Henry takes an interest in visiting your friend Daisy, or that Lars guy with his B&B, or the woman at the end of the road with the old cabin, I told him he needs to clear it with one of us first."

I froze. Us. Needs to clear it with one of *us*. "If I'm going to be given veto and approval responsibilities, then I need to know if there are any hard lines that you don't want crossed as far as where the kids visit."

He shot me a quizzical look. "You know the neighbors. I trust your judgment, Kay. Basically, no pedophiles, no drug dens, no houses of prostitution, no alcoholics—"

"Is wine on the porch once or twice a week okay?" I interrupted. "Otherwise you might want to start packing."

He grinned. "Wine on the porch, or the occasional whisky when a murder victim is discovered is perfectly acceptable. I'm not a Puritan, you know."

"Got it. Gardening, baking, and antique hoarder neighbors are in. Those facing felony charges are out."

* * *

SEAN CAME OVER, and both he and Henry were spending the afternoon glued to the Xbox. Madison was outside in the hot tub, texting like crazy and hopefully not dropping her phone in the water. Judge Beck had his papers once again spread all over my dining room table. I was on the front porch trying to knit another hat.

And I was being nosy. Mr. Peter's nephew, Bert, had pulled up to the house sometime when I was on the third increase row and was milling about the front lawn looking lost. Actually, he looked like a man faced with an overwhelming task. He got on the phone and was talking to someone while looking at all the washing machines. When he opened the lid of one, a bunch of wasps came out and he ran around the yard, waving his arms and dancing. I'm pretty sure he was swearing, although he was doing it quietly because I couldn't hear any of the words.

After a while, he hung up the phone and headed inside. I heard a bunch of banging noises, then Bert came outside with a garbage bag and a few boxes and started to go through them. Poor guy. At this rate, it was going to take him forever. By the time I was finished my hat, he had a dozen boxes on the porch, items scattered all around him and very little in the garbage bag. Feeling sorry for the guy, I took my knitting inside and put together some cheese and salami, and grabbed some iced tea.

He was muttering to himself and writing in a notebook when I made my way to the front porch. "Thought you might need some refreshments," I said.

He jumped, then smiled. "Sorry, I didn't hear you come up. Yes, I'd love some. You're Kay Carrera from across the street? I was sorry to hear that your husband passed away. My condolences."

"And my condolences to you, too." I sat the food down on an unopened box and poured him a glass of tea. "I didn't know your uncle very well, but in the last week, I'd come over a few times to retrieve my cat, and to get his opinion on a piece of china that my husband and I had received as a wedding gift."

He took a sip of tea and waved the other hand at the stacks of plates and silverware. There was a terribly ugly pug figurine next to the plates. "I wish I knew what any of this stuff is. I don't know what should go in a garage sale, and what should go to an antiques consignment store."

"Can you call in an auctioneer? They're usually pretty good at evaluating the value of estate goods."

"I'd rather get a handle on what there is first. No auctioneer in his right mind is going to want to come here and spend months going through boxes stacked four-high in every room of the house."

He had a point. And I was getting an idea. "My room-mate's son used to come over and hang with your uncle a bit. I can see if he knows where the more valuable pieces are kept as well as *what* they are."

My suggestion brought a pained look to Bert's face. "I remember when that was me over here hanging out with Uncle Harry. Although back when I was a kid, the place wasn't like this. Back then, he had a few cabinets and shelves in each room and in one of the bedrooms upstairs with his china stuff. He had a workshop out in the garage, and stuff in the shed that he was working on. I'd come here during the summer when my parents were at work and watch him fix things. He'd always serve us lunch on his special plates, and tell me a story about them—where they came from, how old they were. Of course, back then I was more interested in the sandwich than the plate. I'd give anything to have those days back."

I sat down on top of an old microwave, thinking it was more conducive to conversation than hovering over him. "What happened? I mean, Daisy told me about the toaster, but it seems things had gone wrong before it got to the point of throwing small appliances."

Bert picked up a blue and gold patterned plate and stared at it. "I don't know. After he retired, he continued to do some repair work, but eventually there were no customers and the junk just kept piling up. Then he started buying more and more of these plates and figurines and stuff. He wouldn't get rid of anything. We had a huge fight when the furnace needed work. He kept insisting he could do it himself, sending away anyone I hired to fix it. He went three weeks in the dead of winter without heat. Pipes were freezing and everything. I scheduled an HVAC contractor to come over while Uncle Henry was at a doctor's appointment, and the repair guys couldn't even get to the furnace. I had to move two dozen boxes, and the repairmen were still there when Uncle Henry got home. Luckily, they were able to fix it before he chased them out with that sword of his.

"After that, he refused to leave the house. The last five years he hasn't even gone to the doctor or out to buy groceries. He's been refusing to let me inside for years now. I think partly because he was ashamed and didn't want me to see how bad things had gotten."

It was sad. Sad for Mr. Peter and sad for his nephew. I stood. "Do you want me to see if Henry can come over and show you where some things are? He's home now."

Bert nodded. "Thanks. I don't know if you'll let him, but I'd be happy to pay him something to help me sort through all of this stuff. I'm getting a dumpster in tomorrow, and there's a guy coming to haul the junk from the yard next week, although I think it will take him a few trips. I could use an extra set of hands—especially if those hands know the difference between what should go in the dumpster and what shouldn't."

CHAPTER 13

I told him I'd be right back and headed across to my house. Judge Beck was still at the dining room table, his head bent as he made notes on some paperwork.

"Hey, would you mind if Henry worked with Bert, Mr. Peter's nephew, in sorting through the stuff in the house? It would be things like opening up boxes, throwing away things that were obviously trash, then separating what is more yard-sale worthy, and what might actually be of value."

Judge Beck looked up. "I'm not certain he'll have more than an hour here and there until school is out. I wouldn't want it to interfere with either his sports schedule or his homework."

"It's not like Bert is going to have the place cleaned out overnight. How about if Henry just shows him where the things he knows about are located and lets Bert know what he was told about them. Then after school is out, he can maybe spend a few days per week there, or half days, or something like that."

The judge chewed on the end of his pen. "I'd want Henry supervised, not in the house alone. Heather and I are still working out the summer custody schedule, so there might be weeks where he wouldn't be with me to help."

"I'm sure Bert will take what he can get. It will give Henry a chance to explore how much he likes this antique thing. He can even do some internet research on different pieces for Bert."

Judge Beck nodded. "I like that idea. And when he gets bored of all the pottery and silverware, he can go back to being a lawyer when he grows up."

I hid a smile. "Auctioneer or florist. Get used to the idea."

He sighed. "Okay. Tell Henry he needs to work out the payment amount and a tentative schedule, then he needs to stick to it and work hard. I'm expecting him to treat this as if it's his first job."

I hopped up the stairs, oddly excited. This would be a great opportunity for Henry to see if this was a hobby he might enjoy, or possibly a vocation. He'd earn some summer spending money and be able to practice early work skills. Bert could use the help. Actually, Bert needed a whole staff of Henrys.

I found Henry upstairs with Sean, playing some fantasy game where they were looking for treasure and killing ogres. Sean. I remembered that Henry said his friend was more interested in the cookies Mr. Peter served than in the antiques he was showing them, but maybe he'd be willing to sort through boxes and do some of the basic cleanup for pay.

"Hey guys," I said, knocking on the door jamb to get their attention. "Are you at a stopping point in your game? I've got some questions I want to ask Henry."

They paused the screen right before one of them launched an arrow at a large, green, warty-looking creature, then turned to me. "Yeah, Miss Kay?"

I outlined Bert's proposal, as well as the points that Henry's father had made, then waited for the boy's reaction.

He grinned. "I'd love that. Maybe I can take my laptop over so I can look stuff up. I'll write it all down in a notebook. Like cataloguing museum pieces."

"More like an archeology dig," Sean complained. "That place is a mess."

"I like the idea of an archeology dig. Come on, Sean, it's fun. Maybe Mr. Bert will hire you, too."

Sean didn't look thrilled at that idea. "How much? Because I'm not going to sit in some hoarder's house all summer opening boxes for a few dollars."

"Just a few hours here and there," Henry pleaded. "I'm sure it won't all be plates and bowls and stuff. Mr. Peter did have that cool sword you liked."

"He showed you the sword?" Not that I thought Sean snuck over and stabbed my neighbor, but the mention of the murder weapon had thrown me.

"Yeah. It was pretty cool. I think he said it was a replica of something people used in Renaissance Italy. A rapier. We took it into the kitchen where there was more room, and Mr. Peter let me try to stab a melon with it."

The stabbing-melons-in-the-kitchen story was making me nervous. "Did you guys take it back up front when you were done or leave it in the kitchen?"

"Oh, we left it in the kitchen. Mr. Peter said he needed to clean the melon juice off the blade."

"See?" Henry elbowed his friend. "That was fun. What if he's got more swords? Or maybe one of those old video game systems? I'll bet if you find an Atari, Mr. Bert will let you have it as part of your payment for helping."

Now *that* got Sean's attention. "Do you think if we found an Atari, it would be working? Lots of stuff at Mr. Peter's house didn't work."

"And lots did," Henry told him. "Remember the toasters? They all worked. Kind of, anyway. There were things he fixed up years ago and meant to sell, but never got around to it."

All this was making me wonder how much time Henry really *had* spent at Mr. Peter's house.

"Shall we go over now? Mr. Bert would really appreciate it if you can show him where his uncle kept the more valuable items and what they were."

Both boys got to their feet and I led the way down the stairs and across the street. Bert was still on the porch, his food and tea finished. As we approached, he looked up from a glass vase. There was a smudge of dirt across his forehead that made him look as if he had a particularly menacing unibrow and line of dark grime smeared from his mustache to his ear. I introduced them, and the man shook each boy's hand.

"Know what this is?" Bert picked up the vase he'd been holding and extended it to Henry. The boy took it and turned it over in his hands.

"That's Fostoria Americana. Mr. Peter had a lot of it. He was trying to complete a set he got from an estate auction twenty years ago." Henry looked up at the man. "Are these boxes from the front room?"

Bert nodded. "Just inside the front door. I thought I'd start there and work my way back so I had more space."

"Most of what's in the front room are recent purchases," Henry told him. "He'd stack them there until he was able to go through them and put them with the others. Except for the display case and bookshelf. Those pieces he rotated, showing off his favorite ones."

Bert stood and we followed him in. "These?"

"Yeah." Henry frowned. "He must have been in the middle of changing them out because these empty spaces used to have knife rests."

I felt suddenly chilled and looked up, noticing that the

shadow was back, this time in the corner where there previously had been none. "Do you think he just hadn't gotten around to putting new pieces up here? How long did it take him to replace stuff on the shelf?"

And had someone, namely the murderer, stolen these?

Henry lifted his chin, narrowing his eyes as he thought. For a second, his resemblance to his father was striking. "When I saw him rotate these displays, he always replaced the pieces he removed right away. But maybe he got interrupted."

I knew what he meant—maybe Mr. Peter got interrupted and died before he replaced the pieces. But I still was concerned that we could possibly be looking at a theft. I'd scoffed at the idea of someone robbing a hoarder, but maybe I was wrong. What if the person knew that Mr. Peter rotated the display of his favorite pieces in these cabinets in the front room? It would be a lot easier to snatch things off these shelves than wind through a maze of boxes stacked four-high to find a treasure to take. That would be like finding a needle in a haystack, but these items were right here, by the front door in plain sight.

People who knew they were here included a delivery person who had to step inside while Mr. Peter signed for something, or a repair person, or... I looked over at Bert. Although why would he steal?

"Why does a man proudly display a few pieces every week or two in a room that's cluttered with junk?" Bert waved his hand in frustration. "Who would see them? He had no visitors, beyond you two boys and Mrs. Carrera, evidently."

"I think he just liked getting some things out and seeing them," Henry replied.

The shelf was dust-free, which was a miracle in this house. I wouldn't have known pieces were missing if I hadn't seen the shelves before with every square inch covered.

"Do you know where he kept the knife rests?" I asked, curious to see if they were back in their boxes, or if robbery somehow played a role in the murder.

"No, but he had some faience in an upstairs bedroom that he said was important. Some of it was Quimper pottery, but he had some older pieces from other makers, too. He claimed there was a silver soup tureen that was really valuable in the basement, but I didn't ever see it. He said the steps were dangerous. He'd need to fix them before anyone went down there.".

I immediately envisioned something that was the equivalent of a priceless Ming vase in a dirt-floor basement next to eighty cases of drain cleaner and a rotted wooden staircase.

Bert looked taken aback. I wondered if he was imagining the same thing. "Let's go upstairs first and see this pottery. Then, if you don't mind, I'd like to check for this vase in the basement while you all are here to call for an ambulance if the staircase gives way under me."

At his words, the shadow detached itself from the corner and headed, unimpeded by the stacks of boxes, to the right side of the house. We had to follow Bert through the winding maze, me bringing up the rear. The stairs were equally difficult to negotiate as they had towers of papers and books on each tread—magazines, newspapers, old bills, and even sale fliers. I brushed the dust off one and wasn't surprised to see it was a circular from a five and dime dated twenty years ago. Wow, I'd forgotten how inexpensive three-subject notebooks were back then.

"The third door on the right," Henry called. Bert pushed a heavy box aside and opened the door. Actually, he tried to open the door, and discovered that it was stuck. Putting his shoulder into it, the man managed to push it open wide enough for us to enter.

The room was floor-to-ceiling with storage tubs and

boxes. A few looked like they'd fallen over, and four boxes were open and empty, the cardboard tossed aside along with crumpled tissue and newspaper.

"They're gone," Henry said, his voice low with shock. "Gone. They should either be on the shelves downstairs or in the boxes here."

"He wouldn't have moved them to another room?" I asked.

The boy shook his head. "No. Everything had a place. It looks disorganized, but Mr. Peter had a system and knew where everything was. He knew exactly what he had, which box in which room he kept it, when he bought it, and how much he paid in addition to the history of the item. It's how he was."

"Do you think you could write down what was up here?" Bert asked.

Henry shrugged. "I could try. I remember a few pieces that I thought were kinda cool, but the rest…I don't know."

"I'd happily pay you to do an inventory of what you saw— describe each piece, list what you remember Uncle Harry telling you about it, where it was located, when you saw it last. That sort of stuff."

The boy nodded. "I can do that."

Bert sighed. "Thanks. Now, let's tackle the basement. Keep those cell phones handy, finger on the emergency button, just in case."

There were a few new treads on the wooden stairs heading into the basement, which made me realize that Mr. Peter really had been trying to fix things and keep his head above water. Sadly, it was a losing battle.

"They're safe," Bert called up. "Come on down if you want to."

Before I could say a word, Henry was down the stairs,

Sean following him and muttering something that sounded like "there better be a sword down here".

There wasn't. There wasn't much of anything down there. It was surprising, given that the rest of the house was stuffed full. Had Mr. Peter just not gotten around to filling up the basement as well? Was he holding off on storing things down here until he'd fixed the steps?

"Is there some stuff back in that corner?" Sean asked, clearly still hoping for a sword or two.

Bert walked around and pulled a few hanging chains, filling the basement with light. That's when we saw that the stuff in the back corner was a collection of rakes and shovels. Beyond a washer and dryer that, I hoped, actually worked, there wasn't much else in the basement. Old paint cans. A stack of wood and trim leaning up against a wall. A broken window.

A broken window. Why would Mr. Peter fix the treads on his stairs and not at least nail a board over that? Or clean up the glass on the floor? I walked over and looked at it closely while Bert and the boys were checking to see if the soup tureen was in an old cooler or a metal locker.

Glass wasn't the only thing on the floor. The basement was dirty, and there were obvious somewhat cleaner square marks on the cement floor that showed where boxes had until recently been placed. I thought of Mr. Peter with his arthritis, how he'd most likely unpacked the items he wanted wherever he'd stored them and carried them individually to the display shelves rather than attempt to lug a seventy-pound box of china down, or up, stairs.

I walked over to the other set of stairs—the ones that went to the back yard as opposed to the interior ones. Reaching up, I pushed on the wooden doors, expecting them to be either stuck as the one off the dining room had been, or padlocked. I nearly fell over in shock when it swung easily open, clattering loudly as the wood door smacked against the backyard patio.

The noise got everyone's attention.

"You might want to call and file a police report," I told Bert. "I'm pretty sure that soup tureen, along with a lot of other things, has been stolen."

"Mr. Peter was afraid of that," Henry told us, his voice wavering. "He'd heard noises at night and told us that there were valuable antiques here."

But he didn't install decent locks on the door, or invest in a security system. All the money he'd spent on his hobby, and he hadn't bothered to secure these precious items.

"He was going to buy a security camera," Sean chimed in. "He said that it came with the delivery of those salt shakers last week."

Bert and I exchanged a puzzled glance, then we all followed him upstairs, looking around the ceiling for any sign of the security camera.

"I opened all the boxes closest to the door," Bert said. "It wasn't there. So I'm assuming he at least unpacked it."

Where would Mr. Peter have put the camera? He was in his eighties, and had arthritis. I couldn't see him climbing up a ladder to mount them up near the ceiling.

There was no security camera, but there was an old video recorder on top of the fridge. Unlike most of the things in the house, it wasn't covered in an inch of dust.

I waved Bert over and pulled the camcorder down, rewinding the footage. Then I hit play. After ten seconds, I started fast-forwarding the tape. It was mind-numbingly boring. There were long stretches of darkness, the only illumination the numbers on the wall clock. Mr. Peter shut it off each morning, then clicked it on each night. From this video footage, I wouldn't have believed that there was a theft if I hadn't seen the empty basement, and had Henry's reassurances that there were things missing from the house. I was about ready to call it quits when a blur of motion appeared on the camera.

"Wait. Back it up. What was that?" Bert asked.

I looked over to the kids who were looking through the contents of a box in the other room, then rewinded the tape, hoping that I wasn't about to see a murder. As much as I wanted to see Mr. Peter's killer caught and prosecuted, I didn't want to see the actual crime in all its horrible details.

It was dark. An odd sweeping light came into the kitchen, and right behind it was a man holding a cell phone. He was a tall, thin man, well dressed, with light-colored hair in a man-bun. I held my breath, my suspicions confirmed as the man turned around and the edge of the cell phone light caught his face.

The intruder on the video recorder footage was Will Lars.

CHAPTER 14

*O*nce again there were police cars on our street, only this time they were out front of the Lars's house. Kat's eyes were puffy, and she had a trembling hand clasped over her mouth. Will was pale and defiant as he spoke with Officer Adams. And half the neighborhood watched and listened in because this was all happening right on the front lawn of their house.

"You need to come down to the station," the officer insisted, not for the first time. "At a minimum, we can arrest you for breaking and entering. But Mr. Peter's nephew thinks there are items missing from the house, so you might be facing theft charges at some point. Four nights of footage are on this tape, and you're the only one on it besides the homeowner."

The officer hadn't mentioned the gigantic gorilla in the room—that Will might be under suspicion in the murder of his neighbor. The video footage ended the night before Mr. Peter died .No doubt it hadn't yet been turned on, as Mr. Peter hadn't retired to bed. Still, Will had been in the house, and, given their prickly relationship, I doubted he was there late at night with permission.

But in spite of the incriminating evidence, I just couldn't see Will Lars as stealing from his neighbor. Unless he was trying to drive the man to a psychotic break by sending his paranoia over theft into overdrive and get him committed, I couldn't see a motive. Will wouldn't have wanted any of the things Mr. Peter collected. And I couldn't see him hauling boxes of things from the basement in the middle of the night.

Of course, I couldn't see him stabbing an old man with a sword, then shoving it through a box either.

"Why, Will?" Kat wailed. "Why were you in his house? What were you trying to do?"

Her husband, for a brief moment, looked both guilty and ashamed, then he straightened up to his considerable height. "I was returning some mail. We'd gotten it by mistake, and he wouldn't answer when I knocked. The door was unlocked. I just wanted to put it on the kitchen counter."

Even though I couldn't see his face, I could imagine Officer Adams's expression. "We really should do this down at the station, Mr. Lars."

Both Kat and Will ignored him.

"Oh, for goodness sake, Will," Kat shouted, taking her hand from her mouth and waving a finger in her husband's face. "You couldn't leave the mail on his front porch? Or put it in his mailbox? Or let the mailman redeliver it? What. Were. You. Doing?"

Will sighed, smoothing back a lock of blond hair that had come loose from his man-bun. "I just wanted to see inside. He never let me in, and the complaint I made to the city health and safety inspector had fallen on deaf ears. I thought if I could find a collapsed ceiling, or mold everywhere, or eighty dogs in filthy cages, that they might *do* something about the guy."

I'd been sympathetic toward Will's dilemma, but he'd really crossed the line. Let's just say I was glad that he wasn't living next to me where he'd no doubt have complained about the overgrown herb garden, the untrimmed hedges, and the hot tub that had sat like a piece of junk in my back-yard until last week.

"Do you want to press charges?" Officer Adams asked Bert. The man looked from the police to Will, shifting from foot to foot nervously. No one wanted a neighbor on his bad side, especially when the house would remain unoccupied until Bert could get it all cleaned up and listed for sale. Still, Will was, at the very least, guilty of trespassing, possibly breaking and entering, and potentially theft or even murder.

"No. I mean, if there are things missing…"

"Then that's a different matter," the officer told him. "Right now, I'm just asking about the breaking and entering."

"The door was unlocked," Will insisted.

"Entering," Officer Adams amended. "And potentially breaking and entering, because he might be lying."

Again, I couldn't see Will picking the locks, and the door didn't look like it had been forced open. Maybe Mr. Peter forgot to lock it on occasion, or maybe the lock was so bad that a little jiggle of the handle popped it open. If so, then Bert really needed to look into additional locks.

"No, I don't want to press charges," Bert finally said. The neighbors watching from the sidewalk heaved a collective sigh of relief. Or disappointment. It was hard to tell which emotion was prevalent.

Officer Adams nodded. "I'm still going to need you to come with me, Mr. Lars."

Will's eyes widened. "Why? I answered your questions. I'm not going down to the station."

"I would like to have your fingerprints, to exclude you from the other crime."

Kat gave an involuntary cry at the officer's words. Will reached out a hand to her and she backed away from him.

"I didn't kill that man," Will said. "I wanted him to clean up his yard, or move into a nursing home, or sell his house. I didn't want him dead."

Officer Adams held out his hand, ushering Will toward the waiting squad car. "Good. Then you will no doubt be happy to give us your prints so we can check them against the murder weapon."

Will hesitated a second, then walked down the porch steps, sliding into his car. We watched him drive off, following the police car, then turned to see Kat stomp inside the house and slam the door.

The neighbors made their way back to their houses. Bert locked his uncle's house and climbed into his sports car to head back home. I walked across the street to Judge Beck, who stood with his two kids and Sean, watching the drama.

And a few hours later, as I sat on the porch at sunset with my oh-so-familiar ghost by my side and the newer one occasionally visible prowling among the old washing machines in Mr. Peter's yard, I saw Kat Lars haul a suitcase out of her house and into her car, burning rubber as she backed out of the driveway and headed down the street.

CHAPTER 15

"*M*ake sure you zoom in close to her face when she tells me about her husband," J.T. instructed. I was manning the camera today. Well, one of them. The other was on a tripod to get a second angle so that my boss could cut and edit the video footage like a pro. Actually, I was hoping that soon he would hire an actual pro, or at least a college student with a video major, so we could all get back to work.

"Daisy, stop looking at the camera. You're breaking the fourth wall."

Breaking the fourth wall wasn't the only issue this dramatic reenactment suffered from. I'd been told twice that my hand-held shots were too shaky and that the lighting wasn't optimal. Given that this was an office, not a Hollywood set, and J.T.'s only film experience was a book he'd picked up a few weeks ago, none of this was surprising.

"It's my husband, Gator," Daisy exclaimed, waving her hand about as if she were a proper nineteenth-century lady about to succumb to an attack of the vapors. "He's cheating on me, I just know it."

I zoomed in on Daisy's distressed expression. She was actually pretty good—better than most our police force who usually served as our unpaid actors. I'd need to ask her if she'd done theater in her youth.

The case we were "filming" was an unusual one that J.T. had worked eight years ago, before I'd begun working with him. What had originally seemed to be a spouse with a mistress turned out to be a spouse with a side job. He'd been working a part-time night-shift janitorial job, saving up to buy a hunting lodge that he and his buddies were looking at in Pennsylvania. The hunting trips were an annual event that his wife tolerated, and he knew she'd not be pleased about the purchase that would increase the frequency of those trips as well as the duration. J.T. had felt a bit sorry for the guy, and let the man know he had been found out, which gave Mr. Hunting Lodge a chance to use his second-job earnings to book a cruise for their upcoming wedding anniversary instead.

My boss had revealed the job to the wife, keeping quiet about the hunting lodge part. The woman was overjoyed. In fact, she was so overjoyed that she said if he wanted to keep working the part-time job, he could turn the garage into a man cave for him and his friends. It wasn't a hunting lodge, but he seemed happy with the compromise.

I had no idea if other than changing names and some of the circumstances, J.T. had gotten any kind of signed releases for the subject of this video. That wasn't my job. Filming wasn't my job either, and I hoped that today would be the last time I was behind, or in front of, a camera.

J.T. ran off to download the video and start editing. I poured coffee for Daisy and myself and eyed the large stack of Creditcorp files I had waiting for me.

"So is Will Lars about to be charged with murder? And how long do the police think the robberies at Harry Peter's house have been going on?" Daisy asked, perching on the corner of my desk. I'd gone to bed before Will made it home, but his car had been in the driveway when Daisy had come over for morning yoga. Noticeably, Kat's car had not.

"I don't think he murdered Mr. Peter. And I'm pretty sure that the police don't think so either."

I did wonder if the thefts that had cleaned out Harry Peter's basement had been going on for a while. Ours wasn't the sort of neighborhood where someone could pull a truck up to the curb and haul boxes out to it without being noticed, even in the middle of the night. So, whoever had been breaking into Mr. Peter's house had done it regularly, taking only what he could carry, then making his way to one of the busier streets where he'd probably parked his vehicle. That meant he'd most likely carried the boxes for at least five blocks. And he'd taken the whole box rather than pulling the contents from it. Mr. Peter wasn't the sort to get rid of empty boxes, and there were none in the basement.

And Mr. Peter had clearly realized, most likely when he'd repaired the stairs, that he was missing quite a lot of items from his basement. Had the thief ventured upstairs that fateful night of the murder after taking practically everything that wasn't nailed down from the basement? Had Mr. Peter caught him that night, confronted the man, only to get stabbed?

The stairs had probably been unsafe for quite a while, but Henry's visits had spurred my neighbor to fix them.

"As for the robberies, they could have been happening for months," I told Daisy. "And most likely were only brought to light during the recent repairs. I don't know why Mr. Peter didn't report it to the police when he fixed the stairs and found everything in the basement gone."

"Maybe he was killed before he could," Daisy conjectured.

"Maybe he knew the thief and wanted to handle it himself rather than involve the police."

I'd thought about that. If the thief was a family member, like Bert, or a minor, I could see where Mr. Peter wouldn't want to involve the police, no matter how upset he would have been over the loss of his…stuff. But if Will was the thief, which seemed so very unlikely, I'm pretty sure Mr. Peter would have called the police right away. It made me realize that he must not have checked the video recorder that last night, or Will would have found himself in hot water last week.

I held out my hands palm outward. "I don't know if he knew the thief or not. That could be, or maybe he didn't feel like he could trust the police and wanted to handle it himself."

That made me think. For all his eccentricities, Mr. Peter had seemed a self-sufficient man. After months of broken stairs to the basement, he goes to fix them only to realize everything down there has been cleaned out. Instead of locking the cellar door and fixing the window, he leaves them as is and just repairs the stair treads. Then what? He waits to confront the thief himself, an eighty-year-old man against someone who was probably much younger?

Daisy snorted. "Right. What would I do? Well, I would have called the police the moment I saw that broken window, then invested in a security system, and a really large dog."

Me, too, but Mr. Peter was a hoarder. Would the police even believe that stuff had been stolen, that there had been a robbery in a house where every step was like a game of Twister around boxes and piles of stuff? A broken window could be anything. They'd take the report and do nothing. But if Mr. Peter had set up a video recorder and unlocked the door coming up from the basement to the house, he could have recorded the trespassers and gotten the police to take him seriously.

"Well, I'm sorry the guy was murdered. I hated all the old appliances in his yard, but he seemed like a nice guy. Well, outside of nearly braining his nephew with a toaster, that is." Daisy shifted the stack of Creditcorp files on my desk so she could scoot further over. I was never going to get to them. At this rate, I'll need to come in Saturday and try to catch up.

I shivered with a sudden chill, and tensed, knowing what was coming next. A shadow materialized in the corner of my vision. This time he was even more person-like, with a short, squat body and an actual face, although the features were blurred. I turned my head and the apparition vanished, only to appear again when I looked back at Daisy. Just like the other shadows, this one was only visible if I didn't look directly at it.

"Are you listening at all to what I'm saying?" Daisy complained.

I wrinkled my nose and smiled apologetically. "Sorry. No, I wasn't."

Daisy shivered and rubbed her arms. "What the heck...? Did J.T. suddenly crank up the AC or something?"

She felt it, too? Could she see the shadow? Daisy didn't seem to notice anything off in the corner. But if she felt the chill, then maybe *she'd* believe me.

"Daisy, do you believe in ghosts?"

She blinked in surprise. "Sure. Why?"

My mouth fell open. Sure? Everyone else psychoanalyzed me, and Daisy just said 'sure'?

"Um, because ever since I had my cataract surgery, I've been seeing ghosts."

She pursed her lips and gave me a short, sharp nod. "How many? And are you seeing them everywhere? Because with all the people who have died over the centuries, that would add up to a whole lot of ghosts."

I couldn't believe I was having this conversation. I couldn't believe I'd waited three months to *have* this conversation with Daisy. "At first it was just one ghost, mostly in the evenings, but occasionally during the day. I think it might be Eli. It's the one that's around me the most, that seems to appear when I'm reminiscing, or upset, or lonely. My ophthalmologist said it isn't due to the surgery, although that's when I started seeing them. Reverend Lincoln thinks I'm imagining it because of my grief. The other ones are the murder victims. I saw one near where I found Caryn Swanson's body, I think where she was murdered. And I saw one in Mr. Peter's house when I found his body. I only saw Caryn's, briefly, but Mr. Peter seems to be appearing more often."

I slumped in my chair with relief. To have Daisy so easily accept what I was telling her, to not have her look at me like I was some pitiful creature who was deep in grief, felt like a liberation of my soul. I *was* deep in grief, but unlike the others I'd spoken to, I believed these ghosts were a part of something else.

Well, except for Eli. Eli's ghost probably had a lot to do with my grief.

"Spirits linger, and some people are sensitive to their presences."

"But I've never been sensitive before," I argued. "This came out of nowhere, right after my cataract surgery."

"Which was right after Eli's death," Daisy countered. "You were emotionally vulnerable. You had a surgery that restored your 'sight'. These things probably opened a doorway in your mind that had previously been closed."

"Can I close it again?" Although I wasn't sure that I wanted it closed. I'd gotten used to the Eli-ghost. Actually, I found his presence kind of comforting. The others could go, though.

"Probably not. The second sight might go away eventually, or you might always have this ability. Thankfully you're not seeing every single ghost out there. Some psychics can hardly walk to the corner store without dozens of ghosts materializing in front of them."

I wouldn't leave my house if that were the case. Taking a deep breath, I decided that I might as well get Daisy's thoughts on what I was dealing with here. "So why do some ghosts appear more than once in different locations, like they're following me around? And why don't they speak, or look like actual people instead of shadows?"

Daisy made herself comfortable on my desktop. "Sometimes the spirit is just a psychic impression, usually due to a traumatic event or a strong personality that left an imprint behind when he, or she, died. Those are the ghosts that just repeat the same actions over and over, and tend to remain in the same location. Eventually they dissipate, although in the case of a violent death, they can remain for centuries."

"Mr. Peter is going to be following me around for centuries?" I doubted it since I'd hardly be alive for centuries, but the thought was still disturbing.

"These repeaters don't follow you. They're usually not even aware of your presence, they're just doing their thing over and over and over. Other ghosts are impressions that seem to retain some kind of sentience. Those ones usually want you to do something. In the case of poltergeists, either they want you to move out of the house and leave them alone, or notice them and treat them like houseguests, or roommates. Some want you to find an item that meant a lot to them and do something with it, or bring to light an important event, or discover their murderer."

Now we were getting somewhere. Caryn Swanson's ghost

was clearly a repeater. Mr. Peter wanted something from me. I was guessing he wanted me to find his murderer, but given the man's obsessive interests, maybe he wanted me to find some Polish pottery in the shed before his nephew mistakenly threw it in the dumpster. Eli... "So, what would the Eli ghost want?"

Daisy winced, and suddenly she was looking at me with the same expression that my ophthalmologist and Reverend Lincoln had when they'd spoken with me. "Oh, honey. I think Eli feels bad, and he's tethered here because of unfinished business."

I suddenly felt like there was a grapefruit lodged in my throat. "I'm holding him here. I've clung to his spirit because I didn't want to let him go."

Daisy reached out and grabbed my hand, squeezing it firmly. "No, he's made himself stay behind because *he* feels he left things undone, or unsaid. He was a man who was trapped inside a broken body and a broken brain, but death frees us all. And free, he realized there were things he wanted to communicate, or that he needed to help you transition, that he owed you the comfort of his presence for a while longer. He was not the sort of man who'd rest easy leaving you suddenly after a car accident, or after ten years of being a changed person. It's not you who holds him here, Kay, it's Eli himself."

That did make me feel better. Daisy left soon after, and I got to work on the Creditcorp files, ignoring the spirit that I was sure was Mr. Peter as he lingered around the filing cabinets. He was still there after J.T. had left for the day and I was wrapping up my work.

"I don't know what you want," I told him. "I helped your nephew. We discovered the theft. There was nothing on your video camera besides what I'm sure was just an idiot lapse of judgment by Will Lars. The police are investigating your murder. Bert will take care of any items he knows have been stolen. There's nothing for me to do."

The ghost didn't appear to move, or even acknowledge my statement.

"I wish you'd left some sort of inventory," I told him. "If you had a list of what you had in the house, where it was stored, and maybe even receipts showing where you got it and how much you'd paid, then finding the thief, and probably the murderer, would be a whole lot easier."

There was a thump behind me and I turned to see that the salt shaker had fallen over, spilling white grains across the table and onto the carpet. The hair went up on the back of my neck. Had the ghost done that? They'd never done anything that I could call poltergeist activity in the past. Maybe the salt shaker had just fallen over on its own.

I righted it and wiped up the spill, and when I turned around, the ghost was gone. For a moment I felt guilty, as if I'd let him down. But there was nothing more for me to do.

Actually, there was more for me to do. I could continue to help Bert. I could assist Henry in research and in his efforts to document what he knew of Mr. Peter's collections. And I could be nosy. Two things were very clear in this whole mess. Somebody had been stealing from my neighbor, and the person with the best motive and opportunity to kill him was that thief. But who? Who would know about the contents of a somewhat paranoid hoarder's home? Who would have the nerve to repeatedly burglarize the house of a man who never left his home? And who would, upon discovery, decide to ram a sword through an old man rather than just flee the scene, killing him and jamming the weapon into a nearby box in what I could only think of as a fit of rage? Who?

CHAPTER 16

"What's this?" Daisy pulled a stack of papers over toward her. We'd finished up our sunrise yoga and were eating gingerbread muffins and drinking coffee. Judge Beck hadn't made it downstairs yet. In fact, I hadn't even heard him moving about or the shower running. I wasn't sure if he'd overslept the alarm or was going in late today, but I wasn't about to wake him. The poor guy had been up late both Sunday and Monday night trying to play catch-up now that the kids were with Heather. I was starting to worry about him. If I saw that he was skipping dinner again tonight, I was going to fix a plate and take it in to him. Meatloaf. I'd had a craving and had bought extra ground beef so I could have leftovers for lunch on Wednesday. Even sharing with my roommate, I should still have enough.

"That's Henry's research. Heather brought it by last night so I could give it to Bert. He's taking this job very seriously." And I was so proud of him. Whether he decided to become a professor, an auctioneer, or a lawyer like his father, this boy was going to go far.

"Is this the stuff that was stolen?" Daisy flipped a few pages.

"No, it's an inventory of what Henry remembers seeing, along with what Mr. Peter told him about the pieces. The hope is that Bert eventually finds all of these things in the house, and that any theft was confined to whatever was in the basement."

I doubted Bert would be able to recover any of that. Without any knowledge of what was in the basement before his uncle's death, he wouldn't be able to report anything stolen.

"And pictures, too." Daisy pointed to one. "I actually like these. They're some kind of blue Delft plates."

Quite a few were pretty, although I didn't feel any urges to go buy antique china and pottery from looking at the pictures. The report had to have been fifty pages long. Henry had been very thorough, and I was sure Bert could use it to cross reference what he was sorting through over there. Henry had even noted down the locations where he'd been shown each piece.

"I saw these up front on the display shelf when I was there," I told Daisy. "Henry said they're knife rests."

She laughed. "I don't even think the fancy country clubs use knife rests anymore."

"They should. Balancing my knife across the side of the plate is always a dicey proposition. And I never feel right propping it up on the edge of the plate or sitting it on the table once I've used it."

"We should bring them back into fashion," Daisy announced. "From now on, at every meal I will include knife rests in my place settings."

"Pretty fancy for paper plate cookouts," I teased. "And what about Chinese take-out?"

"I've seen chopstick rests. Yep, I've made up my mind. If you see any knife rests at MegaMart, pick me up a set."

"I'll ask Bert to keep an eye out. I'm sure he'll be happy to sell you a set. Or I'll check at Swanson's. I'm heading there on my lunch hour to see if they'll buy that pitcher on the dining room table." I really wanted to get rid of it before Taco knocked it over and smashed it on the floor.

I managed to get in to work an hour early, Judge Beck staggering down for coffee in his pajamas as I was leaving. J.T was out all morning meeting with bail bond clients, so I was actually able to make a dent in the Creditcorp files. My to-do stack was half the size it was when I left work yesterday by noon, so I didn't feel bad at all about leaving J.T. a note and heading into Milford to unload an ugly pitcher and hopefully return to work several hundred dollars richer.

It was about twenty minutes into Milford, then another ten to find parking during the lunch rush. I was glad I'd gotten in to work early today, because this lunch hour was most likely going to stretch into a lunch hour-and-a-half, if not two. Swanson's Antiques was in a Phillimore Street row house that looked small from the front façade, but stretched back for the entire width of the block. The front section of the store was packed with furniture. Large paintings covered every wall. I walked through the first two rooms before I found the storekeeper standing behind a glass counter with a very modern cash register on top. Outside of the bell that announced my presence as I opened the door, I doubt this guy would have known I was here since he had no visibility to the front part of the shop. Although I guess he'd probably hear if someone was trying to shoplift a fainting couch or an oak armoire.

The man behind the glass counter looked exactly as I suspected an antiques dealer would look. He was thin and pale, as though he spent all of his time in attics and the dark recesses of the shop. His wire-framed glasses were so old-fashioned that the word spectacles immediately came to mind. He looked nearly as old as some of the antiques he was selling, and the few wispy strands of white hair on his head had slid off his comb-over to dangle over his left ear. I could never let Judge Beck meet this man or he'd be shoving Henry toward law school faster than I could bake a scone.

"Can I help you find something?" He smiled, and I blinked at how it transformed his face into 'kindly grandfather' from "emaciated, ghostly-pale horror-movie villain antiques dealer'.

"I'm wondering if you'd be interested in purchasing this." I shifted my huge purse/briefcase to the side and put my box on the counter, pulling out the pitcher. The man made several appreciative oooh-ahh noises. They were much better than the noises Judge Beck made when he'd seen it, or what I'd involuntarily made when I'd unwrapped the gift after my wedding.

"Rostrand. Probably made anywhere from eighteen seventy to eighteen ninety from the pattern and mark. Nice condition." He eyed me and adjusted his glasses. "I can give you fifty for it."

I hated this pitcher. It was ugly and I wanted to get rid of it. But I also had a hot tub repairman to pay.

"I was told five hundred." It was a gross inflation of what Mr. Peter had informed me the pitcher was worth, but I figured I needed bargaining room.

The shopkeeper recoiled dramatically, reverting to 'emaciated, ghostly-pale horror-movie villain antiques dealer'. "Perhaps I could go as high as seventy. It's an unusual item that would take me a while to sell. I'd need to actively solicit to find a buyer, and then there's my mark-up. I could probably only sell it for one hundred if I were lucky."

Liar, liar, pants on fire. Well, I could play that game, too.

"I've been looking on the antique auction sites, tracking actual items sold, and in the last three years, six of these have sold, fetching between two and five hundred U.S. dollars. The two hundred dollar one had some glaze crackle, where this one is pristine. Now, I do agree it might take you a while to find a buyer at five hundred, but there's no reason you couldn't quickly find one to buy this at four hundred. Your offer before shows you're willing to make a thirty-dollar profit on it, but I'll be generous and assume a fifty-dollar profit. Pay me three fifty, and it's yours."

He narrowed his eyes behind those wire-rimmed spectacles. "One fifty."

"Three hundred."

"One seventy-five."

"Three hundred."

"That's what you said before," he complained.

"Yes. Three hundred. That's a hundred-dollar profit for you."

"Two twenty."

This was fun, and I was pretty sure if I hung out and continued to barter with the guy I could probably get my three hundred, but I had to get back to work. And I had a parking meter that was probably close to expiring at this point.

I sighed. "Two fifty and you throw in that set of knife rests." The ones that I was darned sure weren't worth seventy-five dollars.

He hesitated a moment, then nodded. "Deal."

Oh, thank heaven. Because if I had to go home with this pitcher, it was going right up in the attic. The shopkeeper pulled the knife rests out of the case and I admired them as he was writing up the bill of sale. They were three inches long, a hand-painted white glazed pottery that reminded me a lot of the pieces Mr. Peter had on display the first day I'd come over. Each of the five were different, each panel of the knife rest painted alternately with a blue stripe pattern and sprays of wildflowers in a lighter blue and orange.

"I've got more Quimper over there in that case," the man told me. "A coffee pot that matches these with bleuets and a Bretonne woman painted on the side. There's also a lovely plate set with blue on a yellow décor riche border with a Brittany coat of arms at the top."

I wasn't interested in purchasing more antiques, but it was clear that he'd be a few moments writing everything up, and I did want to see this coffee pot, so I wandered over to the display case. The coffee pot was pretty. I was tempted until I saw the price tag. I didn't need a three-hundred-dollar coffee pot, not when Mr. Coffee worked just fine and I had a vacuum-seal carafe to keep my morning elixir steaming hot for hours. I admired a huge meat platter and some butter dishes, then cast my gaze on the next display case which held three fish-shaped serving dishes, bordered in blue and yellow. One featured a lady holding a flower, another a milk-maid, and the third, improbably, a portrait of George Washington complete with his name and the dates of his birth and death.

I recognized these three serving plates. And they were weird enough that I doubted there were two exact sets within fifteen miles of each other. I stared at them for a few seconds, hardly believing my eyes, then I pulled Henry's papers out of my bag and started to go through them, marking down items that he'd seen in Mr. Peter's house that were also for sale at Swanson's. I didn't know enough about antiques to say for certain if these were the same pieces that had been in Mr. Peter's house last week, but I was positive about the fish-shaped dishes.

"Um, when did you get these serving dishes in? The fish-shaped ones with the two ladies and George Washington?"

He looked up. "Saturday."

"This past Saturday?" I didn't want to rule out that Bert had brought a few items in to sell, just to clear a few things out of the house and get some cash. But Saturday was the night when Mr. Peter had been murdered. I doubted that *he'd* sold them, and I'm was sure Bert wouldn't have been authorized to remove items from his uncle's house prior to his death. If it was Bert who'd removed them, that is.

"Yes. I just put them in the cabinet today."

"Where did you buy them?" I tried to make my tone casual. The guy drove a hard bargain, but he didn't strike me as someone who knowingly bought stolen goods. Either way, I didn't want to seem like I was accusing him of anything, especially since he hadn't paid me for the pitcher yet.

"An estate sale. Some guy's grandmother left him her collection. He's been bringing it in a few pieces at a time as he goes through it. It's mostly majolica and faience, some Quimper but a few Porquier and Malicona He also had a nice Wedgwood tea service, and some Flight and Barr Worcester porcelain. The real shocker was a Louis XV Silver Tureen by Jean-Baptiste-Francois Chéret. So many pieces during that era were melted down for coin. And this was in perfect condition. I normally don't deal in high-end pieces like that, but I knew a guy in New Orleans, and sure enough, he was interested."

I felt sick to my stomach. "How much did you sell it for?"

"Fifty thousand. I thought the guy was going to faint when I told him."

"Do you...do you know his name?" I asked, my mind whirling with the thought that the murderer had been right in this store, hocking Mr. Peter's beloved treasures.

The shopkeeper shot me a narrowed glance. "I get identification from all my sellers, in case there's any issue with authentication. I don't give that information out, though."

Of course not. He would hardly want to have someone cut him out as the middle man of these lucrative deals.

"I'm surprised that there was some grandma in the Milford area that had a fifty-thousand-dollar soup tureen sitting around her house. Did she die recently?"

He shrugged, bowing his head back down to the paperwork. "I think so. He's only been coming around for a few months. He's a young man, too. I wouldn't have expected someone in their middle twenties to have inherited a collection of china and dinnerware, but he said that he was the only grandchild. He doesn't seem like the type who would want to keep fish-shaped hand-painted dishes or soup tureens."

Something moved over in the corner of the room, just at the edge of my eyesight. I watched as the ghostly shadow approached, leaning indistinct hands against the display case. This time when I turned to face him, the ghost didn't disappear.

"Guess in a way his grandmother paid for his college. Or at the very least, a really nice car," the shopkeeper added.

I blinked at his words, and suddenly the ghost wasn't what had my attention. In my mind, I pictured a brand new Mustang with all the options and a young owner who I'd not expected to be able to afford such an expensive car. Mid-twenties. Of course, that didn't mean anything. There were lots of men in the area that fit that age range and had nice cars. But Sean and Henry had been spending a lot of time listening to Mr. Peter talk about his collection. What if some of it had filtered through the cookies and lodged in Sean's brain long enough for him to go home and tell his sister's boyfriend about the old man across the street from his friend who had a bunch of dishes he claimed were worth a lot of money.

Or it could have been Will Lars, although he didn't appear

to be mid-twenties. Maybe this shopkeeper was a poor judge of age and everyone under the age of forty looked mid-twenties to him.

"Did he have a man-bun?" I asked. "Tall, thin guy? I'm just wondering because my neighbor had a death in the family and said she had a bunch of antiques he said he needed to sell now."

"No, this guy had a big swoop of hair on the top of his head. Although please send your neighbor my way." He fished out a card and handed it to me. "I'd be happy to give him an appraisal or look at any of the antiques he's inherited."

I took the card, my mind whirring. Big swoop of hair. Like Flock-of-Seagulls hair. What had Sean said the boyfriend's name was? Dustin or Dillon Buckle or something? Either way, this wasn't something I could handle myself. I signed the paperwork, collected my money and my knife rests, then headed back to work. The soup tureen and other items might be a coincidence, but I was certain those fish-shaped platters were stolen. And for anything to be done about that, I'd need to talk to both Bert and the police.

CHAPTER 17

"*T*he new video's up," my boss announced as he blew into the office and plopped a bag on my desk. I'd held off calling the police, wanting to check with Bert or with Judge Beck, with somebody who could tell me that I wasn't imagining the whole thing, and that the likelihood of three identical fish-shaped plates being in the same area was about the same statistical likelihood as me winning the Powerball.

"Well, aren't you going to look in the bag?" J.T. nudged it toward me. I had an urge not to look in the bag, immediately suspecting there were copperheads in there, or that something equally alarming would jump out at me.

It held a wig. And a scrap of fabric that I realized was a dress—a very tiny dress.

"Please tell me you don't expect me to wear these in your next video," I told him. There were limits as to what I should be expected to do under the 'other duties as assigned' portion of my job description. Wearing a wig and a mini-dress at the age of sixty for my boss's internet video wasn't one of them.

"No, it's for Daisy. She did such a great job playing the

suspicious wife that I'm going to have her portray the mother-of-druggie."

I couldn't wait to see Daisy's face when he told her this. Actually, I couldn't wait to see J.T.'s face when my friend verbally set him on fire.

"Did you get rid of the ugly pitcher?" J.T. asked.

"Yep. And I've got cash and a sweet set of knife rests. A word to the wise—Daisy is going to insist everyone use knife rests at her house from now on, so if you go over for dinner sometime, read up on your etiquette books."

J.T. shot me an oddly hopeful look. "She's inviting me over for dinner?"

I'd meant it in a general, making-a-joke sort of way, but my boss must have taken me seriously. As far as I knew, Daisy had no intention of inviting him anywhere. Was J.T. interested in my friend? They'd known each other since forever, having grown up in the same town, gone to the same school, etc. Was this some long-buried crush from childhood, or did yesterday's filming stir up some sparks between the two? Although I was pretty sure this was one-sided. Maybe.

I could play matchmaker if Daisy was interested. It would be a bit odd having my best friend dating my boss, but I'd deal. I envisioned the two of them together and just couldn't see it.

"I found something else at Swanson's this afternoon." I told J.T. about the fish-shaped platters, the soup tureen, and the other plates and pieces that matched Henry's inventory.

My boss scratched his head. "Bert would have to file the police report since he's in charge of the estate. I don't know how he'd claim that they were stolen, though. For all he knows, they're somewhere in that house. It would be pretty embarrassing to accuse some other guy of theft only to find those platters two months later in a box in the attic."

"I'm sure it's the same plates. I mean, come on, J.T., you

can't tell me there are two identical fish-shaped serving platters with George Washington painted on them in the
county."

He wrinkled his nose. "I guess you're right. You and Bert
file the report. Maybe have Judge Beck's kid confirm that the
stuff is missing from where Peter kept it. The police will get
the name of the guy who sold it to Swanson's and check him
out. At the very least, there should be some proof of his
inheritance-from-his-grandmother story."

"ifty thousand dollars." Bert still had a stunned look on his face. "Why Uncle Harry had something worth that much in a box in the basement is beyond me. Seriously. Who does that?"

I shrugged. "Someone who keeps tens of thousands of dollars of china and pottery in boxes all over his house?"

"We don't know for sure the soup tureen was stolen," Officer Fischer commented. "Neither you nor Judge Beck's son ever saw it. All you had was the word of your deceased uncle that there was a valuable soup tureen in the basement. There's no saying it was this one that sold for fifty grand. There's no saying there even *was* a soup tureen in the basement. For all we know, your uncle sold it, or threw it away, or got confused and thought he purchased something that he didn't buy."

He had a point. "Well, I saw the plates, and I can verify that they're the same."

"But what if they're still here...somewhere." The officer gestured at all the boxes in the living room. Bert had been working all day and there was barely enough room to stand at the moment. Which was an improvement. But at this pace, it would take Bert years to go through all of his uncle's stuff.

A black SUV pulled up to the curb. Henry jumped out and dashed through the maze of old appliances to the front door, while his mother took her time getting out of the vehicle. As she should. With a dress and sandals, there was a good chance she would trip and fall if she didn't take care.

"How can I help?" Henry was breathless, his eyes sparkling with excitement. I was glad that Heather had brought him over with such little notice. I knew it was her week, but this was important stuff. We had a thief—and quite possibly a murderer—to catch.

"Do you remember the fish-shaped painted serving platters that Mr. Peter had on this shelf over here about a week ago? One with a lady holding a flower. One with a milkmaid. One with—"

"George Washington," Henry interrupted. "I remember because I thought the fish-shape was really cool, and the portrait of George Washington was really weird."

"Where did Mr. Peter put them when he took them off the shelf to put the knife rests on display?" I asked.

"In the kitchen."

We all scooted aside and followed Henry as he squeezed through narrow passages toward the back of the house. I hesitated, not thrilled about being back in the room where I'd found Mr. Peter's body. As if the thought summoned him, a shadow materialized off to the side. There wasn't a pathway off to the side, so the shadow was overlaid on a stack of four boxes.

"That poor man." Heather appeared at the doorway. For a second I thought she meant the ghost with the boxes through his torso, then I realized she meant the actual, living Mr. Peter. Poor man because he'd been murdered, or because his house looked like a neglected storage unit?

"Yes," I replied, because either one elicited sympathy. "He was lonely. I'm glad Henry came over and spent time with him the last few months. I'm sure he loved having someone to share his interests."

Heather nodded, but looked uneasy at the precariously stacked boxes. "I agree with Nate that he should have told one of us, or you, about coming over here, but I'm glad he did. Our parents don't live close by. It was nice that Mr. Peter took on a sort of grandfather role for Henry."

I heard a crash and a muffled curse and winced. Bert, Officer Adams, and Henry came back down the path. Henry was still practically vibrating with excitement.

"They're gone! The whole box is gone. And I know what was in there, too."

Officer Fischer nodded. "Your son was a huge help, Mrs. Beck. I'll go talk to Bill at Swanson's tomorrow, and update you in a few days."

"You'll also connect with the detective investigating Mr. Peter's murder?" I asked. I'm was sure our local police were good enough at their job to connect the dots without a skip tracer reminding them, but I just wanted to make sure.

"Yep. The thefts might be connected, or they might not be. Lots of burglaries happen when someone dies. Thieves read the obituaries or death notices, and either rob the deceased's house or the family members' while they're at the funeral. But just in case, we'll coordinate."

Officer Adams left, and the four of us walked out to the front porch where Bert had made more headway and there was actually room to stand in a group as opposed to single file.

"There's one more thing I wanted to show you before you left," I told Henry, reaching into my bag, pulling out and unwrapping the knife rests.

"Yeah. These were in the box with the fish-shaped plates and the other stuff," he said. "Aren't they pretty?"

"Yes." I sighed, thinking that I was now out the equivalent of probably fifty bucks, and Daisy would have to wait for her knife rests. "I found them at Swanson's. It's probably premature, but I'm thinking we've found our thief." And possibly our murderer.

"I'll get some security cameras set up and additional door locks," Bert said. "I haven't seen any sign of a break-in in the last two days. No one has messed with the plywood I put over the broken window last night, or tried to cut the lock of the cellar door, but just in case, it won't hurt to have some additional security."

It was another thing that pointed to the thief being the murderer in my mind. If he was just stealing, Mr. Peter's death would have been the perfect opportunity to come back and really clean the place out. But I'd think a murderer would be reluctant to return to the scene of the crime.

We waved Heather and Henry off, then I turned to Bert and handed him the knife rests.

"Oh no." He handed them back. "You paid for those. I'm not going to take them."

"They're stolen property. You get them back. I try to get my money back from Swanson's, and he has to try to get his money back from the thief. That's how it works."

"Not in my world," he said, refusing to take the outstretched package. "Now, if you had that fifty-thousand-dollar soup tureen, that would be different. I'm not going to take those back, not when you've been so helpful. Not when you're the one who put me in touch with Henry. If it hadn't been for you, I wouldn't even have known stuff was stolen."

He had a point. "Okay. Thank you."

"No, thank *you*. I owe you more than a few knife rests.

Once I get this place cleaned out and organized, I'd like to offer you a few of the plates or vases."

Oh, no way. I suddenly envisioned my house full of ugly pitchers such as the one I'd just gotten rid of. "Actually, I bought these for my friend Daisy. I'm not really into this china stuff myself. We're all still eating off the set of dishes I bought thirty years ago."

"Well, if you see something you like, let me know." Bert's smile crinkled up the corner of his eyes. "And hang onto those dishes of yours. Who knows? Some grandchild might treasure them after you're gone."

I had no children to have grandchildren for me, but for some reason my mind immediately envisioned Henry, remembering me fondly as he admired some item from my house and showed them to his kids. "Yes. You're right. Who knows?"

CHAPTER 19

*J*udge Beck was home at a reasonable hour, once again spreading his papers all over the dining room table. I pulled the meatloaf out of the oven and fixed two plates, both with mashed potatoes, gravy, and green beans.

"Clear a space," I announced, bringing both plates into the dining room.

Judge Beck looked up and blinked at me in surprise. "You didn't have…is that meatloaf?"

"Comfort food. And you look like you could use some comfort." I put the plate down on the cleared spot, then sat at the end of the table, carefully relocating a stack of papers.

He eyed the papers, then my plate. "I'm going to be the worst dinner companion ever. Three bail hearings, two motions, case law research. Oh, and two parole hearings tomorrow that I need to look over."

"And a partridge in a pear tree?" I teased. "Don't mind me. Read your paperwork. Try not to get gravy on your reports."

He smiled over at me. "It's nice not to eat alone. And to eat something home-cooked. I try so hard to prioritize

141

family when I've got the kids, then the week they're with Heather I feel like the wheels just came off the bus."

He was juggling a lot, but soon the kids would be off to college and he'd be missing them. In the meantime, freeing up the weeks that he had custody meant loading double the work into the weeks that he didn't.

"Did I just see Taco out there?" Judge Beck pointed a fork out my window. Dusk was slipping into night, but even with nothing but the pathway lights for illumination, I could clearly see a fluffy cat strolling toward the front yard.

"Oh, no. How did he get out there? All the doors are closed. Is he Houdini cat, or something?" I jumped up and looked around. Was it a different cat? Although with meatloaf on the table, Taco should be underfoot, begging. The fact that he wasn't here made me pretty darned sure that the feline strolling down the pathway was mine.

I ran to the front door and to my porch just in time to see Taco at the curb, tail twitching as he carefully looked both ways.

"Taco," I called. "Dinner, dinner, dinner."

That should get him to come. He'd already had dinner, but from experience I knew that the cat's memory when it came to food was conveniently faulty.

The cat paused, even looking back at me for a moment. Then he took off across the street, disappearing into the maze of washing machines that dotted Mr. Peter's front lawn. Dratted cat. There would be no chicken sandwiches for him across the street. He would have been better off coming to me. At least he would have gotten a bite or two of meatloaf from me.

"I'm going across the street to fetch Taco," I called to Judge Beck before shutting the front door and heading across the street.

It was even darker in Mr. Peter's yard with the light

blocked by the Lars's fencing. The old appliances cast deep shadows across the narrow pathways, tall weeds brushing against my ankles as I made my way to the front porch. Bert had left a light on in the living room, but no other ones were lit either in the house or on the outside, and I stumbled as I headed up the stairs. I'd expected to find Taco waiting at the front door, yowling like he always did when he wanted in at home. Instead I saw the swish of his tail as he disappeared through the front door—the *open* front door.

"Bert," I called, peering through the narrow space into the living room. "Bert, Taco just snuck over here. I'm coming in." I didn't hear an answer. Was he still here? I couldn't imagine Bert not locking up or even leaving the front door open, but I hadn't noticed his sports car out front. Had he left, or was he upstairs where he either couldn't hear me or where he'd take forever to wind his way downstairs?

"Bert?" I opened the door wide and stood in the entrance, looking for Mr. Peter's nephew or my cat. I didn't see either, but I heard a noise from over near the dining room. Darned cat. I was tempted to leave Taco here to be locked in for the night, but I worried about my cat, and I didn't think Bert would appreciate finding that Taco had used the carpet as a litter box or that he'd amused himself by knocking breakable items onto the floor throughout the house.

"Here, kitty, kitty, kitty," I called, making my way through the maze of boxes. The sound in the dining room abruptly stopped and I hesitated, expecting to see my cat come bounding toward me. Taco did appear in the kitchen door-way, but instead of rushing into my arms, the cat turned away once more. I imagined him in there, begging Mr. Peter's ghost for chicken sandwiches.

In fact, I saw Mr. Peter, or rather, the specter I'd come to believe was Mr. Peter's ghost. The shadow knelt down, his arms opened wide as Taco leapt toward him, giving a happy chirp. The fact that he sailed right through the ghost's outstretched arms didn't seem to bother either the cat or the ghost.

Changing course, I went past the dining room and into the kitchen where I found my cat on the counter, eyeing a cookie jar. The ghost had remained, and I'd felt an arctic chill as I'd walked through him, trying to concentrate on my cat. I scooped Taco up in my arms, murmuring a mix of scolding and affectionate statements. And when I turned around, I saw a man.

Not a ghost this time, but an actual living human.

I recognized the young man as the one from the ice cream place with the fancy new Mustang, the one who Henry had said was Sean's sister's boyfriend. Dillon Buckle. He had no weapon in hand, but there was a determined, somewhat resigned look on his face that told me I wasn't getting by him. It also told me that there was a good chance I was going to end up like Mr. Peter, although not by a sword. Strangulation? Bludgeoning? I didn't want to contemplate my probable demise in any detail.

He was in the kitchen doorway, blocking my exit. The door to the dining area and outside to the backyard was inaccessible. And this guy was clearly a trespasser. As was I, but I had come in through an open front door, and I was positive Bert wouldn't have minded me coming in to retrieve my cat.

The burglar-most-likely-murderer took a step toward me, and tightened my grip around Taco. He yowled in protest, digging claws into my hands, and I reacted instinctively, throwing my cat at his face.

Poor Taco. Although, in the split second it took me to push past the man and run for the door, I realized I should be thinking 'poor Dillon'. Taco latched on with claws, then jumped to the side before the man could hurt him, taking a good bit of skin with him on the way. The burglar screamed, swatting in vain at my cat and stumbling into a stack of boxes as I shoved past him. I heard a crash, but didn't look back, my focus on getting out the front door. I knew Taco could take care of himself, both in the ability to hide in this over-stuffed house and to claw and bite anyone who wished him harm. I, on the other hand, was vulnerable.

How vulnerable was made clear to me when I felt someone tackle me not five feet from the door. I smashed into another tower of boxes, these holding heavy enough items that the wind was knocked out of me. A few fell, contents sliding across the open space that Bert had just cleared. I twisted around, trying to get out from under the intruder, only to find myself on my back, his hands coming around my neck.

Strangulation. Lovely. Although bludgeoning probably wasn't preferable in the ways-to-die categories. I bucked and kicked, at first reaching up to grab the man's wrists, then groping around beside me as I realized that I didn't have the upper body strength to pull his hands away from my neck.

The pressure increased and my fingers gripped something smooth and cool, like a handle. Bringing it up, I slammed the teapot as hard as I could against the man's head.

It must have been a very sturdy teapot because it didn't break. It did cause the man's head to jerk to the side. He cursed, his hands loosening on my neck, so I hit him again.

This time the teapot broke. I hit one more time with the chunk I still had in my hand, feeling it rip through the skin of his scalp. Blood poured into his eyes and onto me, and he pulled his fingers away from my neck to swipe at his face. I pushed him, jabbing with the broken piece of teapot as if it were a knife and saw him jerk backward to evade my strike. I kicked my legs up and he fell to the side, knocking yet another tower of boxes over.

Five feet to the door. Unfortunately, in our tussle he'd positioned himself between me and my escape. I prepared myself to act like a linebacker and try to shove past him when I saw two hands grab the intruder by the shoulder, spinning him around. A fist slammed into my attacker's chin and the man went down in a shower of boxes and broken pieces of china.

And now the only person that stood between me and the doorway was Judge Beck.

He shook his hand, grimacing as he rubbed his knuckles. "That always looks so easy in the movies. I think I might have broken my fingers." He extended his other hand down to me. "Are you okay?"

I nodded, letting him help me up. My throat hurt. My shoulder hurt where I'd hit the boxes. Once I was on my feet, the judge turned his attention to the intruder, hauling him to his feet, twisting his arm up behind his back and smashing him face first against the only wall space visible in the room.

"Do you have your phone? Mine's in my back pocket. Call the police and I'll hold this guy either until they get here or we can find something to restrain him with."

I didn't have my phone, and it was with extreme reluctance that I reached into Judge Beck's back pocket to retrieve his phone.

Don't squeeze his butt. Don't squeeze his butt. He's your tenant, and he's twenty years younger than you. Don't squeeze his butt.

I managed to pull the phone from his pants without any untoward sexual undertones and dialed 911, telling the operator in a shaky voice that I'd walked in on a burglary in progress, had been attacked, and that we had the assailant pinned against a wall.

Dillon Buckle squirmed and cursed, trying to get away, but Judge Beck was surprisingly buff for a lawyer. With a calm demeanor, he held the other man pressed against the wall, twisting his arm upward to still him when he struggled. I was impressed. He was a judge, an academic type, and although I thought he was very attractive, I'd never once considered him the sort of man who would manhandle an intruder and restrain him until the police arrived.

It was Officer Adams who was first to the scene, his eyes bulging as he saw Judge Beck pinning a man against the wall. Once Dillon Buckle was cuffed and both the judge and I had given our statements, and once Bert had arrived and we'd once again explained what had happened, the house cleared out. Dillon Buckle was hauled away to be charged with attempted robbery, and most likely actual robbery, attempted murder, and most likely actual murder. Bert locked the door and after expressing his concern and thanks, left once more in his little sports car.

Which left Judge Beck and me in a front yard full of washing machines, directly across the street from my —our—house.

"When you didn't come back right away and when Taco came tearing through the dining room with his fur all on end and his tail like a prickly brush straight up in the air, I worried." He turned to me, but I couldn't quite see his expression in the darkness of Mr. Peter's front yard. What I could see was two shadows, one sitting on a chair, rocking slowly on my porch, the other standing in the glass-enclosed side porch of Mr. Peter's house, his shadowy form partially inside the boxes of toilet paper.

"You saved my life. Thank you." I didn't know why it irritated me that my boss, J.T., had saved me from the mayor three months ago, and now Judge Beck had saved me from Mr. Peter's killer. What was I, a damsel in distress?

He laughed. "Are you kidding? The guy was bleeding and concussed by the time I'd arrived. If someone had told me the first day I'd met you that you were someone who could take down a murderer mayor and a killer thief, I would have laughed at them. You're an action hero with knitting needles, a cat, and silver in your hair, Kay. You're smart and funny, laid back and cool. You have completely won over my two children. And you make a hella-good meatloaf. I'm pretty close to worshiping you at this point."

That brought tears to my eyes, but I blinked them back. "I didn't take down the murderous mayor, J.T. did. And I was astonished. He's totally the Gator Pierson of his videos."

Something odd flashed across Judge Beck's face, but it might have been my imagination. It had been a long and traumatic evening, and the light was very dim here in Mr. Peter's yard.

"Oh. Of course, you've known him a long time. Was Pierson a friend of yours and Eli's? Like Carson?"

The shadow on my porch left the rocking chair and vanished through the exterior wall of the house. I kept staring at where he'd been, thinking of Judge Beck's words and wondering what in the world was happening with my life.

"Carson and his wife are very good friends. Before Eli's accident, we used to go out a lot together. And after the accident, Carson gave me odd freelance jobs to do and both he and Maggie brought casseroles over to the house regularly. I didn't know J.T. until a few years ago. I'd met him through Carson. He needed someone to do research on the occasional risky bail client and Carson recommended me. After Eli had died, J.T. offered me a full-time job as a skip tracer, and I took it."

I saw Judge Beck nod, a lock of his dark blond hair sweeping down across his forehead. "How are you doing, Kay? I mean, I know you really loved Eli. These last three months must have been so hard for you. I can't believe the grief you must be dealing with, and then to add the fiasco with the mayor and this." He waved his hand at Mr. Peter's house.

I glanced once more over toward *my* porch, and saw nothing. Where was he? Where was Eli? I felt on the edge of a panic attack just thinking about the fact that he was gone.

"There are good days and bad days," I told Judge Beck. "Sometimes people fit together like puzzle pieces. Ever since that first date with Eli, I was smitten. And although we had our fights, the love never faded. I feel like half of me has been violently ripped away, that I'll never be whole again. And when the accident happened, I just buried it all and plunged myself into the care of my husband. The man I married has been gone for ten years, and I feel like this is the first time I've been able to surface for a breath, to actually acknowledge his loss and mourn the man I lost that night."

There was a moment of silence when I heard the faint sound of cars from Main Street three blocks away, heard the Simmons's chihuahua yipping from the end of the block, heard the rustle of leaves as a late spring breeze blew through the maples that lined our street.

And I could have sworn I heard Judge Beck's ragged inhalation.

His arm came around my shoulders and pulled me close. I felt his breath against the top of my head. "I'm mourning too, Kay, although it's different for me. Still, I feel like we're walking adjacent paths, heading in the same direction. In three months, you've become a part of my family. Madison and Henry adore you. And you're like an anchor keeping me from drifting out to sea in all the madness of my life. I can't begin to imagine how lost you must feel right now, but know that there are people who care about you. Know that Madison and Henry would be lost without you. That…. that I'd be lost without you."

Family. I recalled Reverend Lincoln's words about how

God sends us who we need, and sometimes those people came and went from our lives, that we needed to have faith in our Lord to always provide us who we needed.

I wrapped my arms around Judge Beck, turning my attention from my porch to bury my face in his shirt. "I love Madison and Henry with all my heart. And welcome to the family."

CHAPTER 20

*O*fficer Adams stopped by our office the next day to tell me that Dillon Buckle had been the one who'd been selling the antiques to Swanson's. And no, he hadn't inherited an estate from his grandmother. Under a plea bargain, Dillon had confessed to theft and second-degree murder, saying that he'd been surprised by Mr. Peter in the kitchen, coming up from the basement to take additional boxes in a robbery. There had been an argument. Mr. Peter had attacked him. He'd grabbed the sword that had been on the counter to be washed after the cantaloupe practice, and stabbed the man in self-defense.

I didn't believe that and neither did Officer Adams, the detective, or J.T. Self-defense, my butt. I could see Mr. Peter surprising him when he came up from the basement to steal stuff, but the fact that he'd shoved the sword through a box after stabbing the homeowner didn't seem like the act of a man concerned with defending himself to me. And he hadn't run away or hidden when I'd entered the house, but instead had attacked me, and had attempted to strangle me. The police were charging Dillon separately with that crime, no doubt hoping to tack additional jail time on the second-degree murder plea.

I'd been slowly going through the stuff in my attic, but sadly I didn't feel comfortable taking it in to Swanson's after I'd identified Dillon Buckle as a thief. The antiques dealer had needed to reimburse Bert the cost of the sale of the soup tureen, plus return all the other items. I winced to think of the money the owners had lost and only hoped that they would be able to recoup some of their money from Dillon. Maybe they could sell his car and recover the money that way.

J.T.'s YouTube videos had gained a respectable following that I was sure wasn't just the local P.D., and he was already talking about optimizing Google ads from his website and other stuff.

Henry's hot tub party had been a big hit. He was doing well in track this year, and Sean and the other boys had really enjoyed pizza and banana chocolate chip cake after their pizza and sodas. Henry was helping Bert go through the contents of Mr. Peter's house, and he was excited for summer vacation.

Madison had helped me make the banana chocolate chip cake, and was already proposing several recipes from my books for her father's birthday the following month. She'd completely abandoned her medical career plans, but was torn between her desire to please her father by going into law and a surprising interest in diplomatic relations.

Taco still wasn't thrilled with his status as a house cat and attempted to sneak out the door every chance he got. He often succeeded.

I worked. I loved my job, and when I came home at night, I was always thrilled to see the shadow lurking around the corners of my house. I was also thrilled when Judge Beck came home with the kids, or he came home alone, dragging a huge briefcase. As much as I adored Madison and Henry, there was something comforting about having the judge there by himself. He might be silent, files spread across the dining room while I knitted, or he might join me for dinner, but either way, his presence was a comfort.

And those nights when I knitted by the lamp light, the shadow that I thought was Eli's ghost by my side and Judge Beck in the dining room, muttering softly as he read through his briefs...those were the best nights of all.

I was truly blessed. And up until this moment, I'd never really felt the comfort of what I'd come to know as family.

CONTINUE the series with Antique Secrets - coming September 28, 2017!

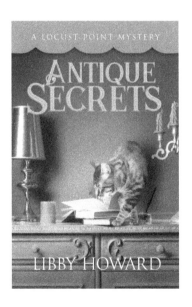

ACKNOWLEDGMENTS

Special thanks to Lyndsey Lewellen for cover design and typography, and to both Erin Zarro and Jennifer Cosham for copyediting.

ABOUT THE AUTHOR

Libby Howard lives in a little house in the woods with her sons and two exuberant bloodhounds. She occasionally knits, occasionally bakes, and occasionally manages to do a load of laundry. Most of her writing is done in a bar where she can combine work with people-watching, a decent micro-brew, and a plate of Old Bay wings.

For more information:
libbyhowardauthor@gmail.com

ALSO BY LIBBY HOWARD

Locust Point Mystery Series:

The Tell All

Junkyard Man

Antique Secrets

Hometown Hero

A Literary Scandal

CPSIA information can be obtained
at www.ICGtesting.com
Printed in the USA
BVHW070115191020
591038BV00004B/447

9 781733 069113